SID PORTER

WILLIAM POST

authorHOUSE®

AuthorHouse™
1663 Liberty Drive
Bloomington, IN 47403
www.authorhouse.com
Phone: 1 (800) 839-8640

Published by AuthorHouse   08/07/2017

ISBN: 978-1-5462-0259-2 (sc)
ISBN: 978-1-5462-0258-5 (e)

Print information available on the last page.

OTHER BOOKS BY WILLIAM POST

The Mystery of Table Mountain

The Miracle

A Call to Duty

Gold Fever

The Blue Ridge

A Doctor by War

Inner Circles

The Evolution of Nora

Darlene

The First Crossing of America

The Tides of War

The Gray Fox

Captain My Captain

Alaskan Paranormal

Some Boys From Texas

The Law and Alan Taylor

The Riflemen

A New Eden

A Soldier and a Sailor

Lost in the Ukraine

Kelly Andrews

A Ghost Tribe

Lost in Indian Country

A Trip to California

A Promise to a Friend

Sid Porter

A Stranger to Himself

Pure Love

A Change in Tradition

Hard Times

The Gathering of a Family

Wrong Place - Wrong Time

CONTENTS

Chapter 1   A Hopeless Love 1

Chapter 2   The Trip to Mexico 12

Chapter 3   The Ramos Ranchero 21

Chapter 4   Mexico City................................. 32

Chapter 5   Gaudalajara 42

Chapter 6   The Prison Riot 57

Chapter 7   Lake Chapala................................ 62

Chapter 8   Back to Mexico City 75

Chapter 9   Lisa Returns to the Ranch 81

Chapter 10   The Trip to Austin.................... 87

Chapter 11   El Paso and South................... 96

Chapter 12   A Trip Postponed...................112

Chapter 13   A Message from Home 126

Chapter 14   A New Home 134

Chapter 15   A Traitor Causes Trouble 147

Chapter 16   A Sea Voyage and Love........... 163

Chapter 17   Living the Good Life 172

Chapter 18   Chanel Perez..................... 187

Chapter 19   A Letter from Monterrey 195

PREFACE

Sid Porter had good parents. They reared him in the West Texas town of Junction. They taught him the things a boy should know like respect for his elders, to think of others before himself, never to lie and that his word was his bond. They also saw that he was in church each Sunday, although they didn't attend that often.

There was a retired army physician who doctored animals, and was very good at his trade. Sid became fascinated with this work, and watched, when he could, how the doctor treated them. The doctor noticed that Sid was interested and decided to teach him about treating animals. From then on, Sid was with the doctor as much as he could be, and learned much about the doctor's skill.

He was twelve, when he first really noticed Mrs. Cook for the first time. He had gone with Doctor Anderson to the Cook ranch to treat a horse. Mrs. Cook came out to the barn and they were introduced. When Sid put out his hand to greet her, she took his hand in both her hands, and gave him a gorgeous smile. Sid was instantly in love.

He began to notice the days Mrs. Cook came into Junction. He was always beside her buggy when it came to a stop, so he could help her down. She liked the attention. She had never had a son and became attached to Sid. They began sitting together in church and later holding hands during the service. She saw Sid as a son, and Sid saw her as the women he loved. She was thirty years older than Sid. Their lives moved on and they finally came together.

The story stretches into Mexico where Sid spends the majority of his life. I hope the reader will feel the warmth of Sid and what made him do the things he did. The story is somewhat of a love story, but with many twists to it.

CHAPTER 1

A HOPELESS LOVE

Sid Porter was born in Junction, Texas. His father was a blacksmith who also owned the livery stable. When Sid was twelve, he was assigned to work as a hostler after school and sometimes at night.

Sid loved horses and the care of them. A retired army doctor, Reeves Anderson, had settled in Junction. He was especially good at treating ailing animals. He had studied horses and cows in college, and specialized in treating them. He had gone through medical school, and then into the army. There he cared for both men and horses.

Sid liked Reeves and was with him when he treated both cows and horses. If Reeves were going out to a farm or ranch to treat an animal, he always came by for his little buddy,

Sid. Sid's father always let him go, because he could see this as good training.

Sid received a marvelous education on the treatment of animals. Once they went out to the Cook ranch to treat a horse. It was there that Sid saw Alta Cook for the first time. She was over forty, but Sid was mesmerized by her. When they met she took his hand in both of hers, and smiled a gorgeous smile that melted Sid's heart.

Her husband, Charles, was always sick, so Alta ran the ranch. Their two girls had married, and were now living away from Junction. Sid began to picture Alta as his make believe girl friend. He saw her as often as he could. He knew approximately when she would be arrive in town, and where she went when she was there. Sid just happened to be at each place where she would go.

Once she said, "My, Sid, we seem to meet each other very often. Then jokingly said, "People may begin to talk."

Sid just smiled and said, "They probably think we're a couple." which made Alta laugh.

Even though it was supposed to be a joke, Sid made the best of it, and often sat with her in church. Alta liked him to do that, as she had always wanted a boy, but just had the two girls.

When Sid graduated from high school, his father and mother talked to him. His father said, "Your mother wants to go back to Boston to be with her mother before she passes on. All of her family is back there. I have decided to sell out and take her home. I hope you will go with us."

Sid thought a minute, then thinking of Mrs. Cook said, "No, I think I'll try to get a job with Doc Anderson. I like it here in the West, and don't cotton to those Yankees."

"Well it's up to you, Sid. You're practically a man now, and must do your own choosing."

Before they left Sid's mother talked with Alta Cook, when she was in town. She explained that they were leaving for Boston.

Before his mother could say anything, Alta said, "I'll hire Sid. He will help me a lot as he knows how to doctor horses and cows. He'll be a big help." She was elated that Sid would be with her everyday now, as he had become dear to her.

She caught Sid alone and told him about her and his mom's conversation. She said, "I want you to work for me, Sid. Lopez left last month, and you could really help us. His sister's husband in San Angelo died, and she needs him badly since her husband's gone. What do you say?"

Sid smiled and said, "I would love to work for you, Mrs. Cook."

"Then it's settled. I will expect you bright and early next Monday. She then said, "There may be talk now that you will be at the ranch," and they both laughed as many people saw that they liked each other. Of course everyone knew Alta was thirty-years older, so no one thought a thing about it.

Sid's heart jumped knowing he would see Alta every day. He called her Alta to himself, as she was his secret sweetheart.

"You will be Rafael Alvarado's partner. You're not prejudice are you?"

"No ma'am. I like Rafael. You don't think he'll think I'm too young do you?"

"No, Rafael is not like that. He'll enjoy teaching you. I'll enjoy having you around me more. We just seem to fit together."

Her statement warmed Sid's heart, as he was in love. He knew it was hopeless, but if he could just be near her, it was good enough.

Sid's folks sold out and left. Sid moved to the bunkhouse at the Cook ranch. Rafael treated him nicely. He said, "Sid, I miss Mexico. I don't have anyone to speak Spanish with since Lopez left. Would you try to learn Spanish, so I can talk my language with you?"

Sid said, "I would love to learn Spanish." From then on they talked mostly in Spanish. Sid picked up the language fast. He turned the sentences around a lot, but soon he got the hang of it. Rafael then began to weed out his Texas accent, and before the end of two years Rafael said, "You talk better Spanish than Lopez did," and they both laughed.

During this time Alta Cook used Sid around the house a lot. She sometimes pretended he was the boy she never had. The other hands began to rag Sid about being a momma's boy. However, Sid took it good naturedly and said, "Are you jealous of me?" and everyone would laugh.

Rafael and Sid rarely went to town. When Sid went, it was always with Alta as he helped her load supplies and do the shopping. Once in awhile she would give Sid a hug that he dearly loved. The longer he was there, the hugs increased. She sometimes kissed him on the cheek when no one was around.

After two years a drought set in and Alta had to cut her herd in half. She called all the hands together and said, "I must let half of you go. The only fair way to do this is the last hired, is the first to go. This meant Sid was being let go.

After paying off the hands, Alta asked Sid to come to the house. He was very sad at leaving the Cook ranch. When he arrived, Alta was dressed in the dress Sid liked the most, and had told her he liked it on her.

Alta said, "Sid, I hated to let you go, as you have become dear to me. But the drought has caused me to cut down and I had to be fair."

Sid said, "I understand. As we may never see each other again, I would like to tell you something. You have always been my make-believe sweetheart. I know we are far apart in age, but you're the only girl I ever loved or wanted."

"My, Sid, I have had the same feeling about you, but I made believe you were my son."

"No, Mrs. Cook, I'm not your son, I'm your sweetheart. I know it's impossible, but I would have loved to be your husband. I know this is embarrassing, but I wanted to tell you before I left. Before I go to sleep each night I always think of you. It has been that way since I first met you. You now know I love you."

Alta said, "Are you leaving at first light?"

Sid said, "Yes, I'm going to Monterrey, Mexico to see Rafael's family. I promised him I would, so they will know he's okay. I also want to visit Mexico. Rafael has told me so much about it, that I want to see it for myself. I will be taking you with me in my heart."

Alta said, "Come here, Sid. He walked to her thinking she would just hug him, but she took him in her arms and kissed him passionately. It lasted awhile and Sid thought he was in heaven.

Alta then said, "When you think of me at night, you will now have that kiss to think about. I will also think about you and the kiss we had. We will probably never see each other again, but we'll be sweethearts forever. You should tell your wife that you had a sweetheart that was thirty years older than you."

"You may be my sweetheart for life. I shall never marry, because I feel you are my wife."

After saying this, Alta kissed him again then said, "Go, Sid. You have stirred up this old lady."

Sid left the next morning before daybreak. He was now hopelessly in love. He had a map with him. He followed the Llano river until it turned west, then he continued south. He pick up the Nueces River, then continued on to Carrizo Springs, the only town between there and Laredo.

The trip was easy as the terrain was mostly flat. He noticed a lot of unbranded cattle, but they were wild and dangerous. He shot a calf the third day at around sunset. He was camped on the Nueces and decided to stay there awhile. He stripped and smoked some of the meat into jerky. It took a couple of days to do this. However he enjoyed fishing in the river, and caught several catfish.

The sixth day out, he saw Carrizo Springs from a butte. He also saw dust from a group of men riding to the town. Sid remembered the words of Alta saying to be extra careful. So, he loosened the girth strap and waited by a creek to let his horse drink and crop some grass that was along the creek.

Sid felt the riders were now in town, so he tightened the girth strap and headed into town.

The town had just one row of buildings. There was a creek that ran through the town and the buildings all faced the creek. There was a road between the creek and the buildings. He could see a ford over the creek about midway and then several adobe buildings across the creek.

As he was pulling up to a saloon he heard gunfire. A man came staggering out of the saloon holding his chest that was red with blood. Another man came running out firing back at the saloon. From instinct, Sid took his canteen and rifle, and in one hop was off his horse. There was a pile of logs between him and the creek, so he ran for it. Bullets were now kicking up dirt beside him, as he jumped behind the logs. He had no idea why they were firing at him, unless they thought he was with the gang who had rode in ahead of him.

He stayed there, and ever once in awhile he heard a bullet hit the logs in front of him. It was dusk now, and Sid thought he would wait until it was dark, then try for the adobe houses across the river. He figured they were Mexicans and he spoke Spanish. His skin was dark from all the time in the sun. His hair was dark brown, so he thought he may pass as a Mexican. However, his clothes would give him away.

It was now dark and the moon hadn't risen yet, so Sid crawled toward the river. It was shallow and he could see it had a road going south with adobe huts on each side of it. At the end, maybe a quarter of a mile away, an adobe sat in the middle at the end of the road.

Sid decided to try for that hut, as it was further than the rest and had a view of the town.. No one fired at him as he kept low to the ground and moved slowly. In less that ten minutes he was there. The door was open as the weather was warm. A Mexican lady said in English, "Come on in, it's safe here. The gringos are back drinking again."

There was a candle burning that barely lit the one room. He gave the woman a smile and said, "Gracious, Senora." He spoke in Spanish and said, "I've been mistakenly fired upon. I just rode into, town and they began shooting at me."

She spoke in English and said, "Si, I saw the whole thing. They think you are one of the Bar Seven riders. It will be impossible to tell them you aren't, as the Bar Seven has many riders. They have intimidated the town until the men of the town decided to fight back. Unfortunately you picked the day to come when that happened.

"They will probably come search for you tomorrow. They are vicious men and will hang you if you are found. Are you hungry?"

Sid nodded and she said, "I am Juanita Sanchez. The gringo's killed my husband six months ago. He worked at the livery stable, and was owed three months salary. Instead of paying him, the owner shot him. He said that Ortiz was stealing from him, so he had to shoot him. They gave me his body. He was shot in the back.

"They don't like me and will probably kill me, too, as they know I saw Ortiz's body before I buried him."

"I will see that don't happen. I have weapons, too, you know."

"Don't try that, Senor. They will only kill you. Here, take a seat and I will feed you some menudo."

Sid sat and said, "I'm Sid Porter, from Junction, Texas. I'm going south to Monterrey to visit a family of a friend of mine. He has been gone over five years, and they need to know he is safe. After that I may go on to Mexico City."

"You need to leave tonight, Senor."

"I can't. They have my horse and saddle. I must get them back before I can go on."

"Then, they will kill you."

"I'm not that easy to kill. You will see."

Jaunita said, "I have but one bed, but you can share it with me. I am still in mourning so I cannot bed you."

Sid smiled and said, "I have a sweetheart. The funny thing is, she's fifty years old. What do you think of that?"

"Nothing. If you love her, and she loves you, it's alright. Age has nothing to do with love. The heart knows who to love."

Sid said, "You are a wise person, Juanita." he then continued eating his menudo which was quite tasty.

Juanita said, "They will not come until tomorrow, so we should go to bed, so we are rested. We may both be dead this time tomorrow. It will be nice sleeping with a handsome young man."

As usual, Sid's last thoughts were about Alta. He wondered what she would say if he told her he slept with a Mexican woman nearly as old as she was.

They were up early the next morning. Juanita kept chickens, so they had eggs and part of a smoked ham she had hanging. About ten the next morning, they saw two men coming and looking into every hut as they walked. They had no respect for the occupants. Sid waited. As they approached Juanita's place, Sid went out back and just around the corner.

One of the men said, "Juanita, if you're hiding a man, we will kill you, too." About that time Sid stepped around the side of the adobe with his pistol drawn. The two men had rifles, but they were pointing down.

Sid said, "If you think you can swing those rifles up before I kill you, go ahead and try it. Otherwise drop them and take your pistols out with your left hand and drop them, too."

The men were startled. One said, "What if we don't drop them?"

Sid said, "At the count of three, I'll kill you where you stand. One…."

Both rifles hit the ground followed by the pistols.

Sid then said, "I'm not with the Bar Seven ranch. I just rode up when the fighting started. I had to run for those logs or you would have killed me by mistake."

One of them said, "Maybe it wouldn't have been a mistake."

Sid then said, "Then I will just kill you and cocked his pistol. The man said, "Wait, we won't do you any harm. We'll get your horse and let you ride on."

"One of you go get my horse. I will keep watch on the other. I'll give you ten minutes before I kill your partner, then I'll come for you tonight."

"You think you're a tough guy do you?"

"Tough enough to kill one of you, now. Then I will burn down your town and kill every man woman and child. You have less that ten minutes, now get!"

It made an impression on them, and one of the men took off trotting toward the town. Sid said, "Pick up their guns and put them in the house, Senora. I will watch this one. By the way, I will be coming back through here. If Juanita is not just like she is now, I will make you very unhappy."

Juanita said, "I have a brother who owns a ranch just this side of Laredo. His name is Juan Valdez. Tell him that I am in trouble. He has many vaqueros, and will not let them hurt me. He will come for me. He will remind Senor Davis, that Ortiz has three months wages coming."

In less than ten minutes the other man came leading Sid's

horse. Sid then mounted and rode on toward the south. The men then got their guns and returned to town.

The journey to Laredo was on terrain that had very little vegetation. Along about dusk, Sid spotted some greenery about a mile to the southwest. He turned his horse and found a spring that he was very glad to see. He spent the night, and continued on the next day before day break.

He could see some buildings and headed toward them. It was Juan Valdez's ranch. He was welcomed. Sid told of the trouble in Carrizo Springs. Valdez thanked him and Sid continued on to Laredo the next day.

CHAPTER 2

THE TRIP TO MEXICO

When Sid arrived in Laredo, he decided to look around for awhile before entering Mexico. He met a Mexican at the livery stable who had a lame horse. Sid looked at it and said, "I can heal this horse if you will let me. We need to give that leg some rest and keep it immobile for a couple of days. They rigged a harness, and kept the leg off the ground. He then rubbed liniment on it twice a day to keep the leg warm. In two days the horse was okay.

The Mexican's name was Ruben Sanchez. They talked for two days and learned much about each other. Ruben said, "I quit my job a day or so ago and was wondering what I would do. You say you have to go to Monterrey, so I will go with you. It is safer for two than one."

Sid was glad to have the company. They purchased

provisions, and started the next day. Ruben had traveled the trail before and was a great help. The trip was just over two days ride, so they left early the second day and arrived there two hours after dark. They decided to put their horses in the livery stable and stay at a hotel. The cost was very little.

Ruben advised him to buy a sombrero and some Spanish pants. He said, "You will be treated differently, because you won't look like a gringo." After buying them, no one thought Sid was a gringo, as he and Ruben talked in Spanish.

The next day Sid inquired about the Alvarado family and received directions to a hacienda just south of town. The hacienda had eight foot adobe walls surrounding the house and grounds. The house itself, was enormous. Sid could tell the Alvarado family was well to do.

Sid and Ruben were invited in and served some cool wine. Sid explained about Rafael and they were all very grateful to hear he was safe. They invited them to stay and he could tell the family dearly wanted them to stay, as they had many more questions to ask about Rafael.

The families father was dead, but Rafael's mother was alive and well. There were three daughters. Two were married and the one who wasn't, looked many times at Sid. Her name was Tina. She caught Sid alone and said, "I want to know all about you. Sid smiled to himself and told about his life from twelve years on. He never mentioned Alta.

Finally, Tina asked Sid if he had a sweetheart. Sid smiled and nodded. He said, "I've loved this woman since I was twelve years old."

She said, "Why didn't you marry her?"

Sid said, "She was married, but her husband died. I was then hired on as a vaquero on her ranch."

"You could have married her then," Tina stated.

"No, our ages were too much apart."

"How old was she?"

"Fifty, when I left her."

"Tina gasped. You were in love with a fifty year old woman?"

"Yes, from the first time I first saw her. I left just two weeks ago, but she kissed me goodbye as we both knew it could never work. I think she loves me too, but it can never be."

"How sad. I have known men who married women half their age, but I have never known of a man who married a woman twice his age."

"She is three times my age, Tina, and I will love her until I die."

"Maybe someone else can make you love her as much. Romance sometimes fades with time."

"I only hope so, but I don't think it will. You would have to see her. She doesn't look thirty-five. She rides like she was born to it and she is beautiful. She has two grown daughters ten years older than me. It's a hopeless situation. Only time can heal me."

"How sad, it pulls at my heart strings. I hate to see someone who loses their love. I have seen it though. Someone loves another and the other does not love them. I have seen it three ways, and none of them get what they want. I think some of love is only lust especially with men. Some men marry and then look for another. I think this is terrible, but I hear of it all the time. Where will you go when you leave here?"

"To Mexico City. I have to see that big city. I may even go to Guadalajara."

"I wish I were a man. I would love to go with you. It sounds so exciting. Is Ruben going with you?"

"No, he is returning to Laredo as his mother lives there and needs him. I think he is well to do, because he doesn't worry about working."

"I, on the other hand, have very little, and must seek work in Mexico City."

"Try the American Embassy. They will need someone who speaks fluent Spanish. How did you learn Spanish?"

Sid then explained about Rafael teaching him. She said, Rafael is a wonderful brother, but has a wanderlust. I'm surprised that he is still in Texas. Does he love Senora Cook, also?"

Sid laughed and said, "No, it's just me. Everyone else just thinks of her as the boss, as she is much older than any of her vaqueros."

"Haven't you had any other sweethearts?"

"No, once I saw her at twelve, I was smitten. I don't know why. She told me she often thought of me as the son she never had, but that was until she kissed me. She had never thought of me as a lover."

"She kissed you on the mouth?"

"Yes, it was a parting kiss. I told her that I had always thought of her as my sweetheart through the years, and always thought of her just before I went to sleep. This somehow pulled her heartstrings, and she kissed me very passionately. We kissed one more time, then I turned and left. She told me she would think of me just before she went to sleep."

"Then she loves you, too."

"No. I don't think she is in love with me, but it did make her think of what could have been except for our age difference."

"How old are you now, Sid?"

'I'm twenty."

"Well, if she were twenty and looks like you say she does, she would have the whole country trying for her hand."

"Yes, probably so."

"I have an idea, Sid. Why don't you kiss me and see if there is a difference. It's just an experimental kiss to test your love."

Sid kissed her and they held the kiss for some time. She pulled away and Tina said, "What do you feel?"

"I feel I still love Alta, but I enjoyed the kiss."

"If I kissed you twenty times in a row, do you think you could feel something for me?"

"I would probably feel lust as I do now, and that is no good."

"Lust is good if you are married."

"But we are not married, Tina. Would you want me, now that you know I love someone else."

Tina tilted her head a little and thought. She said, "I would enjoy the lust part, but I don't think I could live with you, if you loved another."

"You see what I mean."

"Are you coming back through here on your way home?"

"I think I will, but I can't promise. I see what you're leading to. You want to know after a few weeks, would I think of you at night as I do, Alta?"

"She smiled and said, "Yes. I think you will remember that kiss. I have never given kisses to another. You are the first. I

16

hope this doesn't make me like you, wanting someone I can never have."

"It won't, Tina. A handsome man will come into your life, and you will fall madly in love with him, then give him ten children," and they both laughed.

Two days later Sid said his adieus and went on his way. He looked back and Tina was still standing alone now, as everyone else had left. Sid turned his horse around and Tina ran to him and he got off his horse and kissed her passionately. He mounted again and this time didn't look back.

He went through town as he had written a letter to Alta Cook. It read:

Dear Alta,

This is the first letter I have ever written. It is a love letter. I still love you with all my heart and think of you every night before I go to sleep. It's a secret love that we have. I especially think of the kisses you gave me. I even kiss my pillow several time each night pretending it's you.

I am in Monterrey and have visited Rafael's family. They were all glad to know that he is alright. His mother wants him to come home, but then most mother wants their sons around them.

I'm heading for Mexico City and hope to write you there. I hope you think of me as your sweetheart, now, and we can have a secret love.

I love you, Sid

He wanted to mail the letter, so he asked a well dress man if he could direct him to the post office. The man said with a smile, "Is it a love letter?"

Sid smiled and said, "It is, but she's fifty years old."

"That is unusual. I would like to hear your story if you don't mind telling me. I'm a hopeless romantic. I'm having a glass of wine over there," and he pointed. "Will you join me after you mail your letter?"

"I would be pleased to."

"The post office is right there," and he pointed down the street. Sid mailed his letter, and by the time he returned he could see the man sitting at a table on the sidewalk with two glasses and a wine bottle. He joined the man with a smile and said in Spanish, "I'm Sid Porter, from Texas."

The man was perhaps fifty and was distinguished looking. He thrust his hand forward and said, "I'm Senor Estonia Ramos. I'm pleased to meet you. I also love a fifty year old woman, so we have something in common. Please tell me how you came involved with a woman so much older than you."

"It started when I was twelve. I saw her at her ranch while doctoring a horse. She was wearing a beautiful dress that fit her perfectly. I had never seen such beauty before. She looked at me and we held our eyes on one another. She smiled and said, "You're Ed Porter's boy aren't you?"

"I could hardly speak, but nodded and said, 'You are the most beautiful woman I have ever seen.' She smiled at me again and said, 'It's nice to have an admirer, even if it's just a boy. It makes a woman feel loved.'"

From then on, I keep a vigilant eye out for her. I figured

out when she came to town, and was always around when her buggy stopped. I would help her out, and then help her load, when she was through shopping."

"What would her husband say about that?"

"He was never with her. He was sick a lot, and finally died when I was sixteen. She ran their ranch, so it was no burden when he died."

"Didn't she have children?"

"Yes, Two girls, but they married before I was twelve. My parents rarely went to church, but she went every Sunday, and I began to sit by her. She liked it. She told me just before I left two weeks ago, that she pretend I was her son in the days before I grew up.

"When I sat with her in church, she began holding my hand, and it thrilled me. It went like that until I graduated from high school."

"Didn't other people notice you were always around her?"

"Yes, but someone started the rumor that I was her nephew. I never denied it, but never said I was. People then just assumed we were close."

"After my graduation, my folks said they were moving to Boston. I loved my parents, but could not leave Mrs. Cook, because I loved her. My mother told Mrs. Cook they were moving, but that I didn't want to go. She immediately said that she would hire me at her ranch.

"My mother was grateful and told Mrs. Cook that she was glad I would be with her.

"When I was at the ranch, Alta used me at her house a lot. I got ragged by the other hands as Alta had jobs for me that kept me close. She fixed me lunch nearly everyday. I explained to the hands what mother had seen, and told them Mrs. Cook never had a boy, so I guess I just filled in for him.

"The boys never ragged me after that, as they all had great admiration for Mrs. Cook, and saw me as something she needed.

"The drought came and she had to cut down the hands to half. I was the last hired so it was only right that I go first. She called me to the house and told me. She had told me that she wished she could some way keep me, but that it wouldn't be fair.

"I agreed and told her I must go. I then told her I had always held her as my sweetheart and had never gone with any other girls. I told her I had been in love with her since I was twelve."

Senor Ramos said, "That is the sweetest story I have ever heard. Will you come to my hacienda and meet my family. I will not share your story with them as it is private, but I want them to know you as I see you. You are a fine young man."

"I would be pleased to meet them, Senor Ramos." So Sid followed Senor Ramos' buggy to his house.

Unknown to them, two men were watching them. They knew that Senor Ramos was rich, and they had planned to wait and kidnap one of his grandsons for ransom. They thought that Sid was either his son or nephew and knew he would pay the ransom.

CHAPTER 3

THE RAMOS RANCHERO

Ramos' hacienda was much better that the Alvarado's place. Sid could tell that Senor Ramos had great wealth. Sid was introduced to Senora Ramos and their family.

The family consisted of two sons who were grown, married with children. One daughter lived in Mexico City with her husband and family, and one daughter about Sid's age had lost her husband when banditos tried to rob him. Her name was Cloressa. She was comely and Senor Ramos had a plan in mind. If he could get Sid to stay awhile, his Cloressa may work her wiles on him and bring him into the family.

After dinner they sat around and listened to three men who had a string trio. They played several of the Spanish favorites. After that Sid was shown to his room. He slept soundly, but was wakened by a rooster. He rose and washed up as a basin with an ewer was on his dresser. He changed and went downstairs. Many of the household were gathering for breakfast.

They were called to breakfast and as they walked to the dining room, Senor Ramos said covertly to Sid, "I know you like older women, you won't try to steal my wife from me, will you?" and they both laughed.

Sid was placed next to Cloressa. After the meal everyone had something to do and Senor Ramos said, "Cloressa, why don't you show Senor Porter the rancho?"

She smiled at Sid and said, "I would like that, shall we go?"

As they walked, Cloressa said, "I know papa is trying to marry me off, so don't be offended if he tries to put us together much of the time. He's a hopeless romantic. He loves my mother very much. If you will watch, he is always smiling at her, and is very affectionate. We all love him."

"When we met yesterday afternoon, I felt I had known him all my life. I had an instant like for him. When he invited me to his hacienda, I was elated, as I wanted to know all his family."

"Did he mention me?"

"No, he was subtle about that. He is a very wise man. You are very fortunate to have a father with such love. It breeds love to others. He told me you had lost your husband and said it with great sorrow. I think the sorrow was for you."

"Yes, he's like that. I think he felt more sorrow than I did when Octarro was killed. Octarro comes from a very rich family who has ties to the king of Spain. Papa wanted the marriage much more than I did. Octarro was very lustful, and I knew I was not his only woman. He was very handsome. All the women threw themselves at him. I think he loved himself more that anyone. I know I should not talk ill of the dead, but I never loved him. Please don't take this the wrong way. I just wanted you to know, as I feel I can talk to you, as you will be riding on.

"What are your plans for the future, Senor Porter?"

"Please call me Sid and I will call you Cloressa. I have never heard that name. Where does it come from?"

"Spain. My grandmother was named Cloressa. My grandfather inherited a large land grant from the king of Spain, and he came over with his family. My father enhanced it greatly as he is very smart, business wise. I think he saw something in you that he really liked, and at once thought of me. Please don't take offence to it."

"No, I understand fathers wanting their daughters to be happy. However, I have a sweetheart."

"Why aren't you with her?"

"Because it is hopeless."

"Is she married?"

"No. I told your father about it, and I think that is why he invited me. I would like you to get the story from him after I leave."

"It must be sad. My father is very sensitive about love. He sees it as the most precious thing in the world. He literally worships my mother. She loves him to make over her and I think it's great."

"It is. Love is precious and should be tended to like you would a small plant until it grows to be strong."

"That is a very sweet analysis. I shall keep that in my heart when I think of you."

"One thing I would warn you about, never love someone who you know you can never have. That is what I did, and it now rules my life."

"You have now pierced my heart and I am dying to know about your love."

"I cannot tell you. Get it from your father. I don't know why I told him. It was just accidental. However, had I not told him, he probably would not have invited me."

"How is it that you speak Spanish so well."

"I worked with a man called Rafael Alvarado. His family lives here in Monterrey, also. He spent a great deal of time teaching me. It was really the central reason of our friendship as he loves Mexico. I came to Monterrey to let his family know he is okay."

"I know Rafael. He courted me. Father knew Octerro's family, and discouraged Rafael from seeing me. When I became engaged, Rafael left for Texas, and no one has heard of him since.

"You must have been good friends?"

"Yes, he was my best friend. When I was let go from the ranch, I promised him to visit his family to let them know he was safe."

"Had father not been so set on Octerro and his family, I would probably be married to Rafael and had his children. When you return, please tell him I still think of him and want him to return. Tell him about my feelings for Octerro. I don't know if I am in love with Rafael, but I think I could be. I know he was in love with me, because he told me so."

Sid said, "We spent many hours together and he never mentioned you. I think it was because it pained him too much. He could tell I was enamored with Mrs. Cook and told me to not go there, because it would cause me great heartache. I told him I was already there. He didn't laugh as most men would have. He just had a great sadness in his eyes. Now I know why. He loved you, and it brought that lost love to his mind. You wanting him to return is good to know. I have a mission now. I will see that you get a chance at Rafael if you want it."

"I do want it. I now understand a little of your heartache. I will sit with Papa after you have gone. When he tells me your story, I will then tell him my feelings for Rafael. He may see him in a different light, now. He is not so enamored with Octerro's family now, as he has learned much about them. He saw their arrogance, and has little to do with them."

"Remind your father of love, and that it can conquer all, if it is intense enough. Remind him of his love for your mother. Tell him that you think Rafael loves you like that."

That night before Sid went to sleep, he wrote Rafael a letter. He sent it to Alta, but it had Rafael's name on the letter. He wrote it in Spanish so it would be private. It read

Dear Rafael,

I met your family and they all want you to return. I also just happened to meet Senor Ramos. He invited me to stay with them. That is where I met Cloressa. While she was showing me their hacienda, I told her about you. She was very surprised that I knew you. She said that had it not been for her father, she would probably have been married to you and

had your children. Please return. Your future wife
is waiting.

Your compadre,
Sid

Sid included the letter with one for Alta. It simply said:
"I love you."

Sid rode to the post office and mailed his letter. He then
outfitted himself for the trip to Mexico City. When he was
buying supplies he met a Mexican man who apparently was
outfitting himself for travel.

Sid introduced himself and said, "I'm Sid Porter, are you
going to travel?"

"I'm Rico Pintos. I am going to Mexico City."

"I am traveling there, also. Shall we travel together?"

"Si. It will be nice to travel with a compadre. The trail can
be dangerous as there are many banditos about, now. I would
not be traveling alone, but my sister is sick and needs me. I
would take a stage, but I have need of a good horse when we
reach Mexico City."

"Have you traveled to Mexico City many times, Senor
Pintos?"

"Yes, I know the trail like the back of my hand. I know
where to camp and where all the watering holes are. Please
call me, Rico."

"Then you must call me Sid. I am in great company, Rico,
because this is my first trip."

"Are you a gringo, Sid?"

"Yes, I want to see Mexico City. I then may go to

Guadalajara. I have a friend who spoke of Mexico with great pride. He was my best friend, and taught me to speak Spanish."

"He did a good job. You have very little accent. The only reason I thought you may be a gringo is because of your Texas saddle. I see you wear the same clothes as us."

"Yes, I didn't want to stick out like a sore thumb. Thanks for telling me about the saddle. I will see about changing it. I will probably be seeking a job when we reach Mexico City."

"Do you have any skills?"

"Yes, I can treat animals when they are sick or ache. I studied under an animal doctor for six years."

"There is great demand for that skill, as very few people possess it. You will probably do well."

As they were leaving Monterey, Sid just happened to notice two men who were tending to their horses at a water trough acting like they were fixing something about their horses. Out of the corner of his eye he saw them watching them carefully. Under his breath he said, "Don't look now, but there are two unsavory men looking at us. They could be banditos."

"Yes, I noticed them. They will probably be lying for us at Dos Agues. I was attacked there once before. I know just how to handle this, if you will trust me."

"I will surely trust you, because I am a novice in Mexico."

"They will probably let us camp, then when we are asleep, gun us while we are in our blankets."

That night they camped in a nice place. It was near a stream and had firewood available. Talking softly, Rico said, "We can see well enough to hold them off while it's light. Tonight, we will stuff our bedrolls like we're in them, then be on each side of the fire behind trees. They will probably hit us around midnight. The moon is bright enough to see them. Watch the horses. Horses are better than dogs when it comes to alerting you. Just watch their ears. Even if they make no noise, their ears will prick.

Just as Rico had predicted around midnight the horses ears stood up and they were both looking in the same direction. Two men crept into their camp with guns drawn. They quickly fired into the bedrolls. An instant later, both Rico and Sid fired. Both men fell. They examined them and they were both dead.

Rico said, "Let's find their horses. There could have been a third party."

Their horses were tied over a hundred yards away. They pulled them to camp and unsaddled them and rubbed them down. They then went to their bedrolls. In just a few minutes, Rico was breathing easily. Sid was still wide awake. He marveled how Rico could sleep after just killing a man. He thought, *"He probably just viewed it like killing a snake or wolf. I guess they are just like that. I know the world is better off without them, but somewhere they have a mother and kin, too bad. Being an outlaw is dangerous business."*

He then thought of Alta and the sweet kisses she gave him. He knew she loved him, now, and that was enough. He enjoyed writing her letters, and did so each week. She now looked forward to them.

The next day they buried the men. They looked at their wallets so they could send them to their kin, but they carried no names, but did have a great deal of cash.

Rico said, "There are probably warrants out for them and

they didn't want to make it easy for the authorities. If we tell the authorities what happened here, they will hold us until they're satisfied it wasn't murder. I say we just take the horses by a livery stable and say we just found them wandering about. What do you say?"

"I think you're right. I say we just let them go near the livery stable at night so no one will connect us with the horses."

"That's the best idea. We'll do it tonight when we reach Victoria."

They were late getting there, and left the horses untied near the livery. Before they let them go, Sid changed saddles with one of them. He now had a Mexican saddle.

The horses smelled the water and feed and wandered toward the livery, as Sid and Rico left. They decided not to stay in a hotel, so no one would see them in the town. The moon was bright, and they traveled until about midnight. They found a nice campsite, and after watering and rubbing down their horses they turned in. They left after the sun rose the next morning.

Rico had a very nice singing voice and sang many Mexican songs. Sid commented, "Are you a professional singer, Rico?"

Rico said, "Yes, I was with a show in Monterrey, but I know another show in Mexico City that will take me on. My sister was the star attraction until she got sick. She didn't write me of her illness. The person who owns the nightclub wrote me that I should come see about her. She owns a very nice casa in Mexico City with a maid, but a person needs family around them when they're sick."

Nothing else was said about his sister, and he continued to sing some very sad songs.

The next night they stayed in a hotel in Valles. It was a small hotel with no plumbing, but they were able to take a bath at a barbershop. They felt much better and asked a man standing in front of a saloon if he knew a nice place to eat.

He said, "Yes, Mamacita will feed you at her house," and he pointed. They knocked on the door and a large woman appeared.

Rico said, "We understand that you will feed us for a price."

She smiled and opened the door wide. They ate at her table, and each left a two peso when they left. They decided not to go to the saloon as trouble sometimes came in those places.

Three days later around noon they rode into Mexico City. Rico said, "Come with me. My sister, Maria, will want to meet you."

The house was large, but not elaborate. It was quite comfortable though. Rico took him to meet his sister. She looked sickly. After just their introduction, Sid left. Later Rico appeared and said, "It does not look good. I think she has an intestinal problem."

He was right, the next day she died. It was a very sad time as Sid saw many people weeping. He stayed in his room as Rico met many people who came to offer their condolences. While Sid was in his room he wrote Alta a letter. He told of his journey and the death of his traveling companion's sister. He also said he would be seeking work as an animal doctor. He always ended his letters by telling how much he loved her.

The next day he asked about, and found where the only animal doctor worked. His name was Junier Flantonoux.

He was a Frenchman who had lived most of his adult life in Mexico City. He had been educated in France as a doctor, but when in Mexico, only doctored animals.

Junier was very pleased to meet Sid after he told him he was an animal doctor seeking work. Sid explained how he learned the trade and Junier said, "That is the best way to learn. I will employ you, but you will work only with me for awhile, so I can monitor your skills."

Sid liked this as he wanted to learn Dr. Flontonoux's skill.

CHAPTER 4

MEXICO CITY

Dr. Flontonoux was extremely skilled. He was marvelous with animals. He showed Sid how to treat a bloated cow. He had a hollow one-eighth inch rod that was pointed. He showed Sid how to penetrate one of the cows stomachs at a particular place. He shoved the rod into the cow's stomach, and it spewed the most noxious gas Sid had ever smelled. The swelling went down. After a half hour, the doctor removed the rod and filled the hole in the cow with a salve.

He said, "Sid, after you have stuck a few cows you will get the feeling of just how far to pierce the rod. It's a feel mostly. After you remove the rod, always use this salve and don't let the cow eat for two days. Give her all the water she wants, but do not feed her. After two days feed her only milk with sorghum in it for another two days, then she will be okay to resume her regular diet."

Sid watched the doctor turn a calf within the cow and then birth the calf. It was a spectacular event to Sid. Later the doctor had him sticking bloated cows and once he coached Sid to turn a breeched calf within the cow with a happy result.

Sid was learning things he never saw Doc Anderson do. He was fascinated with the skill of Doctor Flontonoux. He set broken bones of dogs, and learned symptoms of various diseases and how to cure them.

Six months after he was in Mexico City, Doc Flontonoux was summoned to the Berdo Ranchero. He didn't want to go and told Sid why.

He said, "Senora Berdo has a thing for me. She is generally subtle about it, but the last time I was there, she caught me alone in her parlor and kissed me a passionate kiss. She is very nice looking, and I knew right away that this could be the end of me. So I will ask you to go. You are equipped with most of my skills now, and I have great confidence in you, Sid. Tell them I am ill and cannot come."

Sid understood the situation and was directed to the ranch, which sat over six miles from town. He was greeted by Senor Alberto Berdo. He explained how Doctor Flantonoux was ill, but that he could handle the work.

The ranch had several cows that were bloated on the spring grass after months of eating hay. It took Sid until ten that night to accomplish his job. He was then shown to a room in the hacienda. He took a bath and put on clean clothes, then went downstairs. A servant saw that he was fed.

Sid was up before dawn and checked on the cows and gave

instructions of how they were not to be fed them for the next two days. He checked the salve on the wounds and they were fine. He then went to the house. The household was having breakfast and he had a place waiting for him at the table. He was introduced to the Senora and five children. They ranged from two to twenty.

Sid explained why he was there instead of Dr. Flontonoux. Senor Berdo said, "You did a fine job. Are you from France also?"

Sid said, "No, I'm from Junction, Texas. My parents live in Boston. I came to Mexico to explore it. I had a friend from Monterrey who told of Mexico's beauty so vividly, that I had to see it. I love your country."

They all smiled and had an instant like for Sid. The oldest daughter was seventeen and handsome. The mother was also as handsome as Dr. Flontonoux had described. She had a glint in her eye that Sid noticed, and knew he should stand clear of her.

The two older boys, Gilberto and Armando, excused themselves as they had work to do. The two youngest also left before Sid had finished eating. Only the Senor, Senora and Gabriela were left.

Senor Berdo said, "Senor Porter, I would like to show you part of my ranch if you are interested. I want you to stay with us until you know the cows will be okay."

Gabriela asked, "May I go, too, father."

"That would be splendid." He then turned to Sid and said, "Gabriela is kept out on the ranch and sees very few people. We will be sending her to school in a month or two. It's boring for a young girl. You will be great company for us, Gabriela." She had a gorgeous smile and it was directed at Sid.

There were three splendid Arabian horses saddled for them. They were about to ride out when a rider came and said, "Senor Ramos, you are needed at the south pasture."

Senor Ramos, turned and said, "Gabriela can show you the ranchero to Senor Porter," and rode off with the vaquero. As they rode away, Sid thought, *"I wonder if he planed this?"*

Sid didn't mind, what better way to spend a day than to be with a pretty girl. They rode through a stand of pines and they became thicker. Gabriela said, "There's a cabin just past this wooded area, where we can have coffee. It's used often by the people of the ranch, and is kept nicely for that reason."

They arrived and it was a cabin, but it was furnished with sofas and chairs. Gabriela fixed coffee, and there were sweet rolls also. They sat on a sofa and Gabriela asked, "Will you tell me about yourself, Senor Porter?"

"Call me Sid, Gabriela. I was born in Texas. At the age of twelve, I went to work for a doctor who treated animals. I liked that work and continued in it until I went to work on a ranch. There I met a Mexican man named Rafael Alvarado. We became close friends and he taught me Spanish. While teaching me, he told me of the beauty of Mexico, and I knew I must see it for myself. I fell in love with it and the friendly people. I have worked for Doctor Flontonoux for the last seven months and have learned much from him. He's a splendid doctor. No finer exits. Your family is fortunate to have him."

"Yes, we know. Mother has a thing for him, I think. Is that why he did not come."

Sid was shocked. He said, "Now how would you know a thing like that?"

"They didn't know it, but I was in the next room and saw her turn the doctor around and kiss him. I could tell he was uncomfortable about it, but did not want to cause an unpleasant scene. He respects my father very much. Father does not treat mother the way he should. He rules her. When that happens, love leaves. I would like to speak to him about treating mother better, but I have no way to approach him."

"Nor should you, Gabriela. Some things should be left alone, and this is one of them. Whatever went on, I'm sure the doctor will be very careful. Your mother is lonely and she wants someone to love. Maybe you should talk to her about loneliness. Tell her you are lonely, even if she isn't. Try to get her to confide in you. You may be able to help her. Never tell her you saw her kissing Doctor Flontonoux. That is just for them. It could ruin your family."

"That is good advise, Doctor Porter. I will be very careful. I love my parents. It will be very difficult to handle this, but handle it I must. I don't know how to handle papa, though. He has to be counseled, though.

"If you will spend a few days with us, maybe you could speak of a man you know who lost his wife because he tried to rule her."

"That could backfire on me, but I believe I will chance it if I get the chance. By the way, do you think your father had it planned for one of his vaquero to pull him away so that we would be together?"

She cocked her head to one side and said, "That same thought passed through my mind as he rode away. He likes you. I think the thought came to him about bringing us together."

"Fathers are like that. It's much better that way than arranging a marriage that neither party may want. That happens quite frequently in Mexico, I'm told."

"Yes, I know it happens. I have worried about that with my father. However, he is wealthy and has no need to marry me off for gain, I hope."

"Well, you don't have to worry about him arranging a marriage with me as I have very little."

"No, you have a great deal. The good Lord has given you a charisma that makes people want to be with you. That is worth much more than wealth. Friends are the most valuable things in the world. I have very few friends, as we live so far away. I hope going to school will help, but I am being sent to a finishing school that is for women. I want to be around men, so I can see the different types.

"Mother was a real beauty and told me she had many boyfriends. Her father liked my father because his family was wealthy. He didn't arrange the marriage, but pushed my mother toward my father. She seems to be desperate. Dr. Flontonoux is nice, but she mostly just wants someone to love her. I feel so sorry for her."

Sid said, "If I have children, I hope my girls are like you, Gabriela. You have a pure heart."

"Not so pure. I think thoughts I shouldn't and don't know what to do about them."

"We all have those thoughts, Gabriela. It is part of the human body."

"Do you have a sweetheart, Doctor Porter?"

Sid smiled and said, "Yes and no. I have only loved one woman in my life since I was twelve years old. However, it is hopeless."

"Is it hopeless because she could never love you?"

"No, she loves me dearly, I think."

"Is she married and is like mother?"

"No, she is not married or has any attachment to another man. She lives alone and runs a ranch. She is a good manager and although not extremely wealthy, she is well fixed."

Gabriela's brow knitted and she then said, "Why don't you go back and marry her?"

"I will tell you if you promise to never tell anyone about this."

With a face of great concern she said, "I promise."

"She's thirty years older than me. I loved her the first time I saw her. She had no boys, so she sort of adopted me. I was always there when she came to town and always sat by her in church. We sat close enough so I could feel her body heat. She held my hand all during the service. Her husband died when I was sixteen.

"Later, when my folks moved to Boston, she hired me as one of her cowboys. However, I spent most of my time at her house helping her with various chores.

She knew I liked her very much, but never dreamed I was in love with her.

"She had to let me go as a drought had cut her herd in half. To be fair I was the last hired, so the first to go. The night before I left, she called me to the house. Knowing we may never see each other again, I told her I loved her, and had been in love with her since I was twelve. She then realized that what I was telling her was true. She had always looked upon me as just her son, but then realized that she loved me also. She kissed me a passionate kiss before I left, and I promised to send her love letters. I do this every week."

"A love like that is torturous. Knowing you could be with her, but can't. It's worse than loneliness. I wish I didn't know about that now. Nothing can be done. You will both go through life loving one another and nothing can ever be done. The only way I see is for you to write her and tell her to sell the ranch and meet you in California or someplace, so you can be together."

"No, it would be the same anyplace we went, and neither of us want to live in isolation. No, it's just a hopeless thing. We will just have to live with it."

"Have you ever had a relationship with a girl your age?"

"Maybe a slight one. A girl in Monterrey asked me to kiss her, so I did. She asked me if I felt anything. I told her only lust, because I was in love with another. She took it okay and said, "I may change my mind if I thought about our kiss for several months."

"I'm now glad you told me that story. I will only seek a man my age who can love only me. Many marriages are not good, but the two live together for life. Either the man is domineering or the wife has no respect for her husband. I have seen it in my own parents. It's a terrible thing, but is part of life."

"We had better get along, Gabriela. We have many miles to cover."

She showed Sid most of the ranch. They had a lunch and only returned when it was dusk. Supper was nearly ready.

They cleaned up and met at the dinner table. Sid was dressed nicely in a Mexican style suit that was popular at that time. It made him very handsome. All had dressed nicely.

Senor Ramos asked, "How did you like the ranchero?"

"I really enjoyed seeing it. Gabriela was a splendid guide. They were entertained that night by a small group of mariachis. The music was nice. They all went to their rooms about ten that evening, as many activities were going on the next day. Sid didn't know it, but Senor Ramos and his wife slept in different bedrooms.

About an hour after all were in their rooms, Sid heard a soft knock on his door. He put a robe on that had been furnished him, and opened the door just a crack. When he did, Senora Ramos pushed past him and said, "I have a terrible crick in my shoulders, Doctor. Will you rub it out for me?"

Sid was shocked but said, "The light is not good in here, follow me to the parlor and I will tend to it. The senora had not bargained for this, but had to follow him. He was now downstairs in the parlor. A servant was kept downstairs all night, so the senoras plans had fallen through.

Sid explained to the servant to bring him some hot towels, as the senora had a crick in her neck and shoulders. He was rubbing her neck and shoulders and the servant was gone getting the towels when the senora turned and put her arms about him. Her robe was open and she was nude. She pressed her body next to his and Sid backed away just as the servant returned with the towels. He asked the servant, who was a young woman, to help him. They placed the towels on her bare shoulders. Once the servant girl looked at Sid with a raised eyebrow. Sid gave no indication that would lead the servant to believe this was anything out of line.

Sid then said to the servant girl. Show the senora to her bedroom and change those hot towel every half hour until midnight then go to bed."

They left, and Sid went to his bedroom and locked the door. It took him until two in the morning to go to sleep, but he still woke early. He went downstairs and Gabriela said her mother had some pain during the night, and would be in her room until noon."

Sid never said anything to anyone. He left after breakfast.

When he returned Doctor Flontonoux asked how things went. Sid said, "They were very nice people and treated me nicely." That's all he ever said about the Ramos family.

CHAPTER 5

GAUDALAJARA

Living in Mexico City was a delight. The doctor and Sid went to a cantina everyday after work. It was an upscale cantina that charged about twice what the others charged for drinks. It kept the riffraff out, and men took their wives and girlfriends there. They met several people there. The doctor was now keeping company with a widowed woman that Sid never saw. The doctor sometimes didn't return at night. All he ever said was, that he went to see the widowed woman.

Sid met his friend, Rico there numerous times. Each time, Rico would have a girl with him and sometimes two. They would have dinner together and sometimes go to Rico's performances. The girls that Rico brought were always young good-looking girls, but were show girls. Rico described them as "Good time girls."

Sid was never alone with any of them although several bluntly told him they wanted to sleep with him. Each time he would say that he had a sweetheart, and couldn't do that. One said, "I can make you forget that sweetheart for awhile if you'll let me."

Sid said, "I bet you could, but then I would have to tell her, and that would not do our relationship any good."

She said, "Why can't I meet someone like you?" Sid never answered.

He went by and visited Gabriela at her school. He even took her to dinner several times. He said, "I would like to introduce you to some of my friends, but I don't want you associating with them. They are not looking for any permanent relationship, and are only interested in their own lust."

Gabriela was introduced to many suitors through her school and soon was very interested in a man. She told Sid about him over dinner one night, and Sid could tell she was in love.

He decided that he had seen all he wanted of Mexico City. He had met a lot of people through his work and had numerous clients. One afternoon at the cantina, Sid said, "Doctor Flontoneoux, I am moving on next week to Guadalajara. I have not seen that part of Mexico."

The doctor said, "I've been expecting this. It will increase my patient load, but I know a young man needs to wander."

"By the way, I will tell you something, now that you are leaving. The reason I have never introduced you to the widowed woman I see, is because there is no widowed woman. Senora Berdo comes to town to see Gabriela, and I sleep with her on the nights she is here. She is much happier now. She demands nothing from me, but my lust. She is a delightful lover. I don't think anyone suspects us, but someday they may. Then Senor Berdo will murder me, although he sleeps with several women himself. Good luck."

Sid went by rail now that the railroad had been completed. He liked the railroad as they had a dining car that served good food. It gave him time to think about his life. He thought of Rico and how he dated showgirls. He then thought of the doctor and Senora Berdo. He would rather have his love without being with her, than to have their love life. It was against God's law. He knew he had lust and at times it was overwhelming, but he could live with that. He had seen how other people led their lives and never wanted to be like those people.

The trip was made in just one day and night. One of the passengers he sat by told him about Lake Chapala that was just south of Guadalajara. The stranger told him that well-to-do Americans and some Canadians were now coming to live near the lake. He said, "It's the climate. It has the best climate in the world, and the native people are warm and courteous. They also work for next to nothing."

Sid said, "How many Americans are there?"

"I expect well over two or three hundred. It's just like America down there. Everyone seems to have money and employ many Mexicans as maids and gardeners at good wages."

Sid thought, *"I must see this."* However, he decided to see Guadalajara first. His train arrived just after lunch. He went to a hotel and asked, "Are there any doctors who tend to animals?"

The clerk thought a minute and said, "I think Doctor Contreras has someone who helps him with that."

After getting the address of Dr. Contreras, he caught a hack and asked him to take him to a hotel near Dr. Contreras's clinic. There happened to be one within a block. He rented a room and put up his things. He took a bath and put on fresh clothes. He then called on Dr. Contreras. The doctor was interested in Sid, as Sid told him of his experience.

The doctor said, "I could use you. The man I have, has very little experience and over half the time I have to tend to the animals myself. Several rich people have cats and dogs that they think more of than their friends or relatives. I will have you tend to them. Come in tomorrow. I will pay you quite handsomely as these people have money and I charge them a premium price."

Sid fell into the work and was quite good at it. He began getting a reputation as he knew animals. One day a messenger arrived and asked to see Dr. Contreras. The messenger told him that his master asked that he come to his casa and treat his dog.

Doctor Contreras told the messenger that someone would be there, and the messenger left. He then turned to Sid and said, "Doctor Porter, Senor Ramirez runs this city. He is very rich and has his men everywhere. If he asks someone to do something, it is not a request it is an edict. Those who don't obey are really sorry they didn't. I'm going to send you, as you need to know this man. He's dangerous, but no one can touch him. He owns all the politician and law enforcers."

Sid reluctantly went. He was invited into a room that was elaborately decorated. He could tell at once it was the dog's room. It was brightly lit and the dog was lying on a bed whimpering. The man standing looking at the dog turned and Sid said, "Doctor Contreras sent me as I look after the pets for him."

Sid could tell that Ramirez didn't like this, but said, "I treasure this dog, so be very careful with him."

Sid first asked, "How old is your dog?"

"Sixteen years."

Sid then examined the dog and could tell immediately that the dog had a tumor in its stomach. He turned and said, "Your dog has a tumor in its stomach and I'm afraid I can do nothing, but euthanize him."

Senor Ramirez said, "What is the meaning of euthanize?"

"Put him to sleep, Senor."

"Can't you operate and remove the tumor?"

"Yes, but it would be terribly painful to your dog, and I don't believe the dog could survive the operation."

"Well, operate, I love that dog."

"It would be much better if I take the dog to our office to do the operation."

"No, get what you need and operate here."

Sid asked for a small table to be brought. He padded the table with a blanket and put a sheet over that. He had his scalpel and other things needed for the operation. He asked, "Do you have a nurse available to assist me?"

Ramirez yelled, "Bring Elena here. Tell her she is to assist the doctor in an operation."

Elena arrived wearing a white uniform. Sid said, "I'm Doctor Porter. Senor Ramirez has asked me to remove a tumor from his dog's stomach. There is little chance that the dog will survive, but that is what the Senor wants. I will need some hot water and many bandages. Can you furnish these?"

"I will see to it, Doctor."

Twenty minutes later all the prep work was done. He asked the nurse and Senor Ramirez to hold the dog as he opened its stomach.

Ramirez held the dogs back legs, but turned his head as Sid made the incision.

Sid removed the tumor and stitched its stomach, and then closed the dog back up.

Sid was amazed that the dog was still alive after he was stitched. Sid stayed as did his nurse and Ramirez. They waited an hour and the dog was breathing easier now. Ramirez left, but Sid and the nurse stayed.

The nurse said, "My name is Elena, I am employed to take care of this dog. I needed the money or I would never have come to work here. The Senor is brutal to people who he thinks wrong him. I hope this dog lives. I can see the Senor being very brutal with us if he does not."

"Why would he be brutal? We are doing the best we can for the dog."

"Yes, but the Senor's thinking is some times skewed. If things don't go the way he wants them, someone generally pays a heavy price."

Sid just shook his head and said, "The first twenty four hours will be critical. I am amazed that the dog lasted through the operation."

Elena said, "I am surprised, also. You have very skillful hands, doctor. No one could have done better."

They were served some food and a fine wine, but they

never left the room. Twelve hours later, Ramirez returned and was quite pleased that his dog was alive. However, while he was thanking Sid, the dog died.

Ramirez was infuriated. He turned and said, "Tell Torrez to come."

Sid had just put his tools in his bag when Torrez arrived with two men. Ramirez said, "Take this man to the prison. Tell the warden he is to keep him until I say for him to be released."

Torrez asked, "What are the charges Senor?"

"He killed my dog! You idiot."

"Elena take the dog and see that it is buried properly."

Sid looked at Elena and she just wrapped up the dog in the sheet and turned and left, happy she was not taken, too. They traveled in a carriage until they reached the outskirts of town. Sid could see a giant stone wall and two very large buildings inside.

They were taken to the warden and Torrez said, "Senor Ramirez has ordered you to take this prisoner and keep him until the Senor says he is to be released."

"What has he done?" asked the warden.

"Torrez said, "He operated on the Senor's dog and the dog died."

The warden just shook his head and said, "Okay."

After Torrez left the warden turned to Sid and said, "I'm sorry, but Ramirez controls everything here. I can surely use you though, our doctor left a week ago, and we have no one to tend the prisoners. We have both a men's and women's prison. The women need more care than the men. You will not be housed with the prisoners. You shall occupy the physicians casa that is next to my quarters. I will notify your family if you wish."

"I have no family, but if you would notify Doctor Contreras of what happened, I would be obliged."

Sid's new quarters were nice. He had a four room house with a maid/cook. The maid was a trustee. She was pretty and had a smile when Sid entered his quarters.

The warden said, "This is Maria, "She's a trustee. She's here because she was a maid for Ramirez and broke a bowl that was his mothers. It infuriated, Ramirez and he told me to keep her until he said to let her go. There are others in here with something that displeased him, but I can't give them all special privileges, so they just bide their time until Ramirez thinks they have been here long enough. Many he forgets, I just let them go after a year. If he asks about them, I tell him they died."

Sid said, "Someone needs to take him down a peg or two."

"Several have tried and were sorry they were born. He is well guarded and pays certain people to tell him if someone talks about him. Some have, and were sorry they were born. He's vicious and so wealthy he can pay many people. He has a secret, which is not so secret, he has an army who surrounds him. No one in their right mind goes against him.

"I will keep you for a year, and if he has not asked about you, I will let you go. Meanwhile, you will act as our doctor."

"I only work on animals, Warden."

"Well, until the prison commission sends me a replacement, which will be at least a year, you will serve as doctor and do the best you can."

"If I run into something major, will you send for Doctor Contreras?"

"It would have to be dire, but yes, if I think you can't perform, I will ask him. I imagine he will turn us down, though. He had a bad experience here once before, that nearly took his life."

Sid didn't ask about the experience. He was too weary. He had been up for over twenty-four hours. He went to his room undressed and fell into bed."

He awoke ten hours later and it was light outside. He started to get up, then noticed that someone was also in his bed. It was Maria. She woke and sat up.

Sid said, "What are you doing here?"

"I come with the house. If I don't sleep with you, then I would have to sleep in the prison where most of the women are lesbians. The warden gave me my choice. The last doctor was old and didn't need me often, but when he did, I submitted."

"I will ask the warden for another bed."

"Don't do that, please. The warden would then have to have an explanation. I will just stay on my side if you don't want me. I surely don't want to go to the women's prison."

"Okay, I will protect you, but I don't like to sleep with other women as I have a sweetheart that I'm true to."

Sid asked the warden to see if there were any nurses in the prison. There wasn't any. He then asked the warden to furnish him with several nurses uniforms, and that he needed three white coats. He also ordered various medical equipment he would need.

One of his four rooms served as a medical office. He would

see women on Mondays, Wednesdays and Fridays and men on Tuesday, Thursdays and Saturdays. He had Sundays off.

When he saw any patient, man or woman, he always had Maria in the room in her new nurses uniform. She was even there when men disrobed. Sid knew he would need a witness if anyone questioned him. Also, it was safer. No one questioned him about this practice. At the end of the day he and Maria would have a cocktail of grain alcohol and fruit juice. They both told their life stories.

Maria had been engaged to be married, but after six months she received a letter from her mother that here fiancé was seeing another woman, as he had heard rumors that she was living with the doctor of the prison.

Sid said, "I can see we both will have to put our lives on hold until we are released."

When Sid saw the women, some had sexual transmitted diseases. He sent for medicine that Doctor Contreras provided. The men were the same. He finally got the diseases under control. It seemed the past doctor did nothing for anyone.

Some of the women came on to him, but he was kind and explained he was married. As they knew nothing about him, they took that as true, and most didn't bother him again.

After two months Maria was told by the warden she could go. By this time she loved Sid, but loved her freedom more. They parted with a handshake as they had never kissed.

The warden said, "Do you want another nurse?"

"Yes, I will need one to assist me. It is safer dealing with the prisoners."

"I will put a list together of people I deem trustworthy, then let you interview them."

Sid said, "Could I get another bed for her if she is to stay in my quarters?"

"Didn't you like Maria?"

"Yes, but we never made love. I was glad she left although I liked her a lot. I knew sooner or later we would have made love, and I have a sweetheart I cannot betray. I have written her I am practicing medicine in Guadalajara. I don't want to worry her with the fact that I am in prison."

A single bed was provided and kept in the room used as the clinic. It looked like just another facility. The eight girls selected were scheduled to be interviewed. They ranged in ages from twenty to thirty-two. Sid asked them to tell their life stories and how they came to be in prison. Four of them could be eliminated immediately. One of them, however, was young, and had been led down the road of crime by her husband who was later shot and killed by the Federallies after a robbery. The money from the robbery had never turned up, so they arrested his wife. She lived miles from the robbery with her mother. Her name was Teresa Lopez before she was married, but she could not produce a marriage certificate, and the priest who married them, was now deceased and had never given them back the license. Teresa had only her mother to verify she was never near the robbery. Not having the money, the authorities needed to prosecute someone, so it was Teresa. She was only twenty.

Sid asked, "Are you romantically inclined to any of the women here?"

She said, "No, but they constantly want me. That is mostly why I am here. I would rather sleep with you than be with them."

"If you are selected, you will not sleep with me. My last nurse never did either. I have a sweetheart."

Teresa smiled and said, "You are a gentlemen. Please select me, I will support you as though you were my husband."

"Do you know anything about the money your husband stole?"

"No. I was never near him after he tried the hold up. I told the court that, but they needed someone to prosecute, and I was the only one still alive. Both his partners were killed in the robbery, and they had no women friends."

"Okay. You have the job. You're the same size as Maria, so put on her uniforms and see if they fit."

She began disrobing in front of Sid, but he got up and left to tell the warden he had made his selection.

Teresa was comely. She even caught Sid's eye. She filled out the uniform much better than Maria. Between patients, Sid would tell Teresa what was required of her. He said, "Your first mission is to keep us safe. Never forget, most of the inmates are dangerous, and will do anything to get away. Some would kill both of us without any remorse. The warden gave me a pistol that is hidden in that pitcher. We never use the pitcher as it is empty except for the gun. Would you shoot someone if our lives are in danger?"

"I would. I look at some of these people as wild animals, and I don't think I would hesitate to shoot."

"If you hesitate, we may be dead. During our time with patients, we know are dangerous, I want you to stand by that pitcher. Go now and stand by it. Then reach in and get the pistol. Do you know how to fire that weapon?"

"Yes, you must cock the hammer, point at your target and pull the trigger."

"Who taught you that?"

"My husband."

"Did you love him?"

"I thought I did, but the more I was with him, I could see he was not who I thought he was. I never dreamed he would hold up the bank. He said he was going to look for a job. We only heard about the robbery after he was killed. He had my name and address on him. They came for me and I guess I have to pay his debt."

"How long of a sentence are you serving."

"Five years. My own mother thinks I had something to do with it and never comes to see me. No one does. I think she told the Federallies something, but I can't prove it."

"You'll have a better life, now. I will treat you like a friend, and we will work as a team. I will teach you how to dress wounds, and do most of the things I do. I hope I can give you a medical education so you will have a trade when you leave here."

"You will sleep in that bed there, and we will be friends. I like to have a drink after the end of the day. We only have grain alcohol and fruit juice, but I like it."

"I will like that, too, Doctor Porter."

"I'm not sure you won't have to bed the next doctor. Maria told me she had to bed the last doctor, but that he was old and didn't bother her too often. If you do, just look at it as training for your future husband."

"She smiled and said, "You always look at the bright side of things. I like that. I'm lucky to be with you."

They saw at least ten patients every day. Some just wanted to talk to someone from the outside, as they thought Sid was employed by the prison. The men all thought that Teresa was employed, also. Some of the women resented her and snubbed her. When Sid recognized that, he explained that Teresa had no choice as the warden selected her. This helped some. All thought they slept together.

One of the women asked Teresa, "How do you keep from getting pregnant?"

Teresa said, "The doctor will not bed me, as he has a sweetheart and only sees me as a nurse." This spread and was now accepted.

About three months later, a prisoner asked Sid to look at his arm. As he did, the prisoner grabbed Sid and was trying to break his neck. Then there was a loud sound and the prisoner stood straight up and fell on his face.

Sid was on him quickly and tried to stop the bleeding, but the bullet had gone through his chest and he was dead. He looked at Teresa, and she was in shock. She just stood there with the smoking gun. She then turned and put the gun back into the pitcher. About that time a guard from the outside burst into the room. When he saw the body looking up at the ceiling, he immediately thought that the doctor had shot him.

He then turned, and went for the warden. The warden had heard the shot and was already headed for the clinic.

When he arrived he said, "What happened?"

Sid said, "He attacked me, and I had to shoot him. He never thought about me having a gun, I'm sure. Had you not given me the gun, he would have killed both of us."

The warden then turned and said, "How did you see this happening?"

She said, "It all happened so quickly. The prisoner tried to attack Doctor Porter, but Doctor Porter was too quick for him, and managed to draw the gun and shoot him. Like Doctor Porter said, 'I'm sure he would have killed us both had not Doctor Porter taken the action he did. He saved my life, and I will be eternally grateful to him."

"He probably saved more lives than just you two, if Crib had gotten out of here. You did a great job, Sid. You are a brave man. Many doctors couldn't have done what you did. I would like to commend you, but you know I can't under the circumstances. I will just report this as a prisoner shot while trying to escape. Only the three of us will know what really happened."

The body was removed and all appointments were canceled for the day. It was three-thirty in the afternoon and Sid broke out the alcohol and fruit juice.

Teresa said, "Why did you tell the warden you shot Crib?"

"It would not help your record if they thought you did the shooting. You will need a clean record."

When they got up to go to supper Teresa came to Sid's side and hugged him and kissed him on the cheek.

She said, "Any more things like this, and I will be in love with you."

Sid said, "You've had too much grain alcohol," and they both laughed.

CHAPTER 6

THE PRISON RIOT

Four months passed and women's side started a riot while they were in the mess hall. Teresa and Sid were sitting at the guard's table. Everyone was fighting. Sid grabbed Teresa and took her to a closet adjacent to their table where the guard hung their coats. It was open on both ends and led to the kitchen.

What they didn't know was this was a planned riot. The women were to start a riot. Then the guards in the men's side would go to help the guards in the women's side. When they left, the men would overpower the remaining guards and break into the armory and arm themselves. They would then go to the women's side and slay the guards and break everyone out.

It worked, too. There was soon a pitched battle between the guards and the prisoners. The prisoners out numbered the guards twenty to one and soon had captured the women's side, also. They now had the warden. They stood him on a table, and put a noose around his neck and hung him.

During this time Sid and Teresa made it to the kitchen. The kitchen was staffed by prisoners who were now in the mess hall watching the warden being hung. In the kitchen there was a place behind the cook stoves where wood was kept. The wood had been used and there was a tarp that was used in the outside to keep rain off the wood. Sid placed the tarp over them and they hunkered down and hid.

Sid whispered, "I think they will all leave soon, as they want to be free."

Their bodies were facing one another and Teresa put her arms around his neck and put her head beside his head.

Teresa whispered, "If we die, I will die in your arms," then put her lips on his neck. Sid was so concerned about his own life, that he was not excited by her at all.

After an hour it was quiet. They had not heard a sound for sometime now. They cautiously raised the tarp and peered out. No one was in sight. They went into the mess hall and saw the warden hanging. They saw numerous guards and prisoners that were lying on the floor dead. They checked each one thoroughly. Ones that might have not been dead at first had their throats cut. It was gruesome site. Many prisoners were lying dead.

"What shall we do?" asked Teresa.

"I think we should go back to our quarters and wait. I would not venture out of these walls for anything. There will be prisoners everywhere and this prison is the safest place I can think of."

Teresa said, "Breakout the alcohol, Doctor Porter. I want to drink to the man who saved my life."

"Well, we are even now. I never thanked you for saving my life."

They had just finished their second drink when they heard horses arriving. Sid said, "Put out the lamp." Teresa moved quickly, and put out the lamp.

Sid said, "Let's go behind the house and see who's coming."

Before they left, Teresa went to the clinic and retrieved the pistol. Sid smiled and said, "You might need that."

They were now behind the house and could see men moving about. There was just enough light to see that the men had uniforms on."

Sid then called out and said, "I'm Doctor Porter. I have my nurse with me and we are alone."

He heard an officer say, "Check them out, Sergeant." A sergeant then came to them and said, "What happened?"

They were now in front of the officer and Sid said, "It started on the women's side. We were eating supper and the women started fighting. I immediately told my nurse to follow me. We hid in the kitchen's woodpile behind the stoves with a tarp over us. We waited maybe an hour, and when all was quiet we came out. We saw they had hung the warden. We checked everyone, then moved over to the men's side and checked all the guards there. If they were just wounded someone came around and cut their throats. All are dead. We thought the safest place would be to just remain here until someone came. That's the entire story."

The officer said, "The bodies will be taken out of here in the morning. What are you going to do?"

"Nothing much we can do, as we have no horses unless you can give us a couple."

"I think that can be arranged. The warden has a buggy you can use, and I'll give you a horse. If I were you, I would wait until morning. There are criminals everywhere. We captured two who were trying to break into a general store to get clothes. We could tell by their prison garb they were from here. They soon confessed that there was a prison break, and we came here to check it out."

"I think you're right. We will leave in the morning. Please leave us a horse at the warden's stable."

They returned to their quarters and Teresa was trembling all over. Sid could see she was scared to the inch of her life. She said, "I'm too scared to sleep by myself. I want to sleep with you."

Sid just thought she wanted to be close, but she removed all her clothes and got into the bed nude. Sid put on his night shirt and got into bed. She said, "I'm still scared, hold me for awhile. She then came to him and their flesh touched and she rolled over on top of him. Sid was in a quandary. He knew she needed him, and he could not deny her. It happened so fast that Sid had no time to protest. They made love until Sid gave out.

She still clung to him the rest of the night. When it was barely light, she was on him again. After that she got up and made coffee.

She said, "I haven't ever enjoyed anything like I did you. You are wonderful."

"Yes, but I now have a guilty conscience. I'm not in love with you, and what we did was pure lust."

"It may have been that, but it was wonderful."

"Get dressed I have a plan. That officer thinks we are hired by the prison. Let's pack up everything we may need from the warden's house. He's got to have money hidden and we need it. We will have about an hour to find the money, and get what we need to get to Lake Chapala. I hear there are many Americans around there. I'm an American citizen, and will just fit in with the people there."

In the warden's house they took it room by room. He had a pair of boots in his closet. Teresa shook out the boots and came across hundreds of pesos. Going through the warden's desk, Sid found a hidden drawer that he pried open. There he found around a hundred gold and silver coins. He bagged that up and was about to leave when he saw the warden's liquor supply. After they stashed the money, they carried out a box full of expensive liquor. They then took his bed clothes and many things he had to eat.

Sid hooked up the buggy to a horse that was left them They pulled away from the prison. As they traveled, Sid said, "They have no paper work on me and you will just be listed as at large. Ramirez will probably thinks of me as with the others who escaped, if he even thinks of me at all. We are in the clear if we can make it to Lake Chapala.

Several miles away from the prison they came to a road block. Sid had his identification showing he was an American citizen. They accepted that, and they were on their way. Teresa was scared stiff, but she saw that Sid had great composure and was not intimidated.

A half mile later, Teresa scooted over and put her head on his shoulder. He smiled and said, "We are in the clear now. I'm looking forward to Lake Chapala."

CHAPTER 7

LAKE CHAPALA

The town was not as small as Sid had thought. Several hundred houses could be seen, although most were small adobes. The downtown area had two streets filled with shops. Coming in he had seen several small farms. He wondered if he could start a clinic there. He decided to stop, when he saw a nicely dressed man. Sid asked, "Is there an animal doctor located here?"

"No, and we don't even have a doctor. We need a doctor badly."

"Well, I'm an animal doctor, but I have treated several humans also. I have no medical degree, but I worked for a medical doctor for a time."

"Well, you will be welcomed by all of us. We don't care if you have a piece of paper that says you can help us. We just want to know if you can."

"I'll set up a practice here, but let it be known that I will treat people only if they are aware that I don't have a medical license."

The man turned to Teresa and said, "This must be your lovely wife."

Sid said, "No, that is my nurse. She is very capable and helps me immeasurably."

Teresa smiled at the man and he smiled a toothy grin. Sid then asked, "Is there some shop for sale or rent in the downtown area?"

"Yes, Claude Sikes just closed his shop. He's decided to go back to the states. He's still there. You see that sign that says 'Goods', that's his shop."

Sid pulled the buggy over to the shop and helped Teresa down. They went into the shop and saw Claude behind the counter.

Sid said, "I'm Dr. Porter and this is my nurse, Miss Lopez. We hear you want to sell out and move back to the states. We need a place to set up my clinic. Would you give us a price?"

Claude smiled and said, "I'm Claude Sikes and you are a sight for sore eyes. I'll give you a great price. I built this place some ten years ago. It cost me neigh onto four hundred American dollars. It has a living quarters in the back that is nice. I'll show you that. He turned and they followed him. Just as he told them, there was a living quarters with two rooms. One had a kitchen and table, and the other was a bedroom with one single bed.

Claude said, "I guess you'll have to get a bigger bed, but other than that, you'll be in good shape."

Claude then said, "Open that door," and he pointed to a back door.

Sid opened it and it led into a bathroom with a toilet, sink and bathtub. There was another door off the kitchen and Sid opened that. He could see a stable and a windmill with a tank.

Claude laughed and said, "You're getting a bargain for three hundred American dollars."

"I can give you but two hundred now, and will send you the other hundred in three months. That's the best I can do."

"Well, you have me. There are no other buyers, so I must trust you. You look like a honest man, so, it's a deal." They then shook on it. Claude said, "I'll be out before noon tomorrow."

"Isn't there some kind of a deed for you to sign over to me?"

"Yes, and I'll do that tomorrow at the town hall."

They took a room at the hotel for the night, and then cleaned up and went to eat. At the dinner table, Teresa said, "You have the money to pay him the full amount, why didn't you?"

"We may need every dime we have getting established. It takes time to build up a clientele, and we have to have something to eat on. Plus there may be property taxes and other things."

"I'm not much of a business woman as you can see."

They had to repaint the inside and clear out shelves and counter tops. It cost nearly fifty dollars getting the place to look like a clinic. They added a wall down the center of the shop to have an examining room and an office. Sid also had to pay a man to paint a sign that said, "Medical Clinic."

Before they were through renovating, several people

stopped by to make an appointment. These were set for the following Monday. Before they were through, they had enough patients for the following week.

Sid explained to each patient that he had no credentials as a medical doctor, He would see them if they understood that he was just a general practitioner. No one cared about credentials, they just wanted help. Sid set his prices like Dr. Contrares had charged.

They had bought another twin bed as Sid would not sleep with Teresa. They still had the practice of keeping their pistol in the pitcher. They both would clean the pistol periodically as neither felt completely safe after the prison riot.

They had been there four months. One day a man came in who had his hand in a bandage. When Sid took off the bandage, he saw that the hand was gone, like someone had chopped it off.

Sid asked, "What happened. The man said, "I was working for a man in Guadalajara and was accused of stealing from him. I did not steal from him, but he thought I did, so he had my hand cut off. I could do nothing. I finally stopped the bleeding. I went to a doctor, but he told me that he was given orders not to help me and didn't want to lose his hand, also. Someone then told me that there was a doctor here, so I traveled here."

Sid examined the hand and there was no infection, so he re-bandaged the wrist and told him to come see him in three days unless redness started appearing.

The man was the last patient of the day. Sid brought out some brandy and poured it into their glasses. He said, "Someone has to stop Ramirez, and I think I'm that someone."

Teresa got a scared look on her face and said, "No, don't do that. You will end up being tortured to death. Please don't do that."

"Yes, he has to be stopped. I'm a cautious man, and will have a perfect plan before I make an attempt. I will trust no one, because no one is trustworthy. I will be gone for awhile, so you will have to take my place here. You can do most of what I do and if you can't, refer them to the doctor in Guadalajara."

Teresa then cried and said, "I will never see you again. You're a dead man if you go back to Guadalajara. It was a half hour after they were in bed before Teresa came to him and she was shaking. Sid soothed her until she was calm.

The next day Sid left with his buggy. He thought about making love to Teresa. He felt terribly guilty. He prayed, "Lord, you know I did it for her. She needed my comfort. I knew it was not right, but she needed me, terribly. Please forgive us."

Their was a small town near Guadalajara. Sid stopped to buy clothes. He bought clothes like the peons wore. He had a large sombrero and white pants and a pullover shirt.

Sid knew an old lady who lived on the edge of Guadalajara. He had helped her a couple of times, and had charged her nothing because she was poor. Her name was Gardera. Sid never knew if this was her first or last name. He just called her Gardera. She lived by herself and had no relatives, and only a few friends from her parish.

Sid arrived at dusk and said, "Gardera, I need a place to stay. Senor Ramirez is after me. Will you help me?"

"Si, Doctor, I will help."

"Tell people I am your cousin and have the bad lung disease with no place to stay. This will keep people away, and also give you an explanation of my being here."

Gardera gave him a corner to stay in. He had a lamp with him, and that night wrote a letter addressed to Senor Ramirez. It said:

Ramirez,

You will die within the next year. You won't know when or how. It could be by poison, or a rifle from some distance or maybe a knife blade when you are in a crowd or even a fire. There is only one thing for sure. This time next year, you will be dead. It will be done by someone close, and that you trust. You need to consult a priest before it is too late.

Sid put the note in an envelop with Ramirez's name on it. That night around midnight, Sid took it to the post office, and put it in a box outside for mailing letters.

The next day he bought a fencepost made from an ash tree. He also bought a wood scraper and an awl. He began shaving the post down to make a bow. He worked on the bow several days until he had what he thought was a good bow. He had some strong cord and was able to string his bow. It was so strong it took all his strength to pull it back. He then began making arrows. He tried his bow and found that he could shoot an arrow a hundred yards.

Sid knew of a store that had a flat roof. It sat about a hundred yards away from Ramirez's house. He brought some oil from their lamp, and put it on a wad of cloth. About midnight, he went to the roof of the store and wrapped the head of his arrow with the oiled cloth and lit it. It took three tries before an arrow went into an upstairs window. It was a vacant room about midway in the upstairs. It landed on a bed. The bed became on fire and spread to the ceiling and walls. Within a half-hour the whole roof was in flames.

The whole house was engulfed before people started yelling. Ramirez was awakened, and barely made it out of the house. Sid watched until he saw the house was going to completely burn.

Ramirez was shaken. He knew he had just had a close call. He called one of his men over and said, "I want to know everyone who was in the house tonight. One of them burned my house down. I want the one responsible."

Sid had left with all his equipment and returned home. Gardera was still snoring as she was when he left. The next day, he hid his bow in the rafters of the adobe.

Everyone was talking about Ramirez's house burning. Many laughed, but made sure others could not hear them.

Sid took a train to Mexico City where he bought a rifle, a fifty caliber Sharps. It was the preferred rifle of the buffalo hunters. He had the person who sold him the rifle to package it so that it didn't resemble a rifle. The rifle had a scope on it, and before he returned he practiced with it. While there he visited a laboratory and asked for some poison. He also wanted knockout drops. He told the man he was buying the drugs to capture and kill some wolves that were killing cattle.

He had disguised himself as an old man so if Ramirez hired a detective later, he would not be recognized as a young man. When Sid returned, he was dressed as a peon and no one took notice of him.

Sid knew that Gardera had a sister in Mexico City, but neither had the money to visit one another. Sid paid her way on the railroad, and told her to stay three weeks.

Ramirez had started reconstruction of his new mansion. In the interim, he had taken over a house near him. He didn't bother to rent it, he just had one of his men go over and tell the owner to leave. He told the owner that Senor Ramirez required his house until his was built. The people left knowing the ramifications of protesting.

Sid watched all the food that came into Ramirez's new dwelling. He talked to a widowed women, who worked in the grocery store that supplied Ramirez with food. She could tell he was young, but she had not had any male approach her for some time. She smiled at him and he smiled back.

He asked, "What is your name Senora?"

"Alisa, Senor."

"My name is Pablo. I am Gardera's cousin."

"Oh, I heard you had the lung disease."

"Yes, we told people that, but it is not true. I offended Senor Ramirez long ago when I was a boy, and we were afraid he might remember."

"Yes, one must be careful when you are around Senor Ramirez. What did you do?"

"I brought him some fruit that I was ordered to do. The fruit was over ripe, but no one knew. The Senor blamed me for it, and I was whipped by one of his men. Ramirez said that he was not through with my punishment, so I left the city for several years."

"My, I furnish the Senor with fruit and melons. He likes a certain melon and I have it checked thoroughly, but I will have a look at it myself before it is taken to him, again. I surely don't want him beating me."

"Not even the senor, would beat such a beautiful woman. You excite me."

"She smiled and came closer. Sid then said, "Would you come to Gardera's tonight. She is in Mexico City. I thought we might have a glass of wine together."

She looked shocked at first, but then said, "I would like that, but it would have to be late so no one could see me going to her casa."

"Do you live alone?" Sid asked.

"Si, maybe it would be safer if you came to my casa. I have a very good wine."

Alisa lived not too far away. She also lived on the edge of town. She even drew Sid a map, as she had paper that she wrapped her fruit in.

That night after ten, Sid came. Alisa had bathed and was dressed in her best and had a scent on that was pleasing. Sid just wore his peon clothes, but he had bathed and his clothes were fresh.

They drank and laughed. The more they drank the more funny everything was. Sid had been there an hour and then stood and said, "I must go before I want to stay too much. He walked close to Alisa and hugged her. Her passion was now intense and she clung to him and kissed him. Sid then turned and left.

The next day he met her at her work, and asked if he could have one of the melons that Senor Ramirez liked. She gave him one, and Sid gave her a peso. She said, "That is too much, Pablo."

Sid said, "It is a token for you, Alisa." As he turned to leave he asked, "Who delivers your fruit to Senor Ramirez's kitchen?"

"I just hire anyone who is around."

"Would you hire me? I need the money."

"Si, I can use you for all our deliveries. My boss trusts me to get our produce from the market to the people."

Sid had brought his doctor bag with him and inside he had a syringe. When he delivered the melon to the Ramirez house he had given it a dose of knockout drops using his syringe.

The next day he posted a letter to Ramirez that said:

DO NOT TRUST ANYTHING YOU EAT. POISON IS IN IT.

Ramirez got the note just before his dinner that evening. He brought his cook in and had him taste all his food before he ate it. The cook took a bit of the melon and smiled, then fell forward on his face. Ramirez concluded he was dead, and told the others in the room to take him to the undertaker. He was now in a panic. Who was after him? It then dawned on him that everyone hated him, and that some of them were trying to kill him. He told his two bodyguards to stay in his room when he slept. However, he couldn't sleep.

His cook woke up at the undertakers, and got up and left. He took the midnight train to Mexico City.

Alisa was telling Sid about a woman who had just hired

onto Ramirez's household. The reason she was telling Sid was that no one stayed long working for Ramirez. The turnover was frequent for a reason. Ramirez thought any woman in his house must do anything he wanted. The new maid was unaware of this and Ramirez wanted her to pleasure him while he sat in his chair. She knew if she didn't, she would go to prison or worse, so she did what he wanted.

She was outraged and was telling Alisa about it the next day. Sid was just behind a wall and could hear every word she said. She had told Alisa in graphic terms. Sid then walked up and said, "What are you going to do. If you leave, he will find you and may have a terrible punishment for you. I suggest you stay on for awhile, and then tell his aide that your mother is ill, and you must go to her. I also suggest you stay as far away from him as you can. Where does he sleep?"

"He sleeps in the large bedroom upstairs in the corner. The bedroom has stairs that come down to the yard. One of his guards said, that since the fire he wanted a quick way to get out of the building should a fire start again."

Sid said, "Never go near that bedroom if he is in the house."

That night Sid went to a place where he had a view of the bedroom of Ramirez. He shot five times into his bedroom. One of shots hit just above Ramirez on the headboard of his bed. He was now totally scared.

Ramirez received another note the next day that read:

YOU WERE JUST LUCKY AGAIN. ONE OF YOUR BODY GUARDS WILL KILL YOU TONIGHT.

Ramirez had a pistol on the stand beside his soft chair and one on the stand beside his bed. As the guards were changing, the relieved guard said something to the guard coming on duty as he walked down the hall. The new guard was now coming in the door. He stopped to answer, but his gun was protruding through the door pointing toward Ramirez. Ramirez thought he was aiming at him, and quickly picked up his pistol and as the guard moved through the door, shot him.

The other guard didn't know what had happened and turned to go back, but Ramirez was now at the door and shot. The bullet hit the other guard in the shoulder so he turned and made it to the stairs. Ramirez shot again, but missed as the guard stumbled down the stairs.

The guard yelled, "Get out of the house. Ramirez has gone crazy, and is trying to kill everyone!"

Everyone left the house as quickly as they could. Sid was bringing the fruit for the day and saw everyone leaving in a hurry. He caught the wounded man and asked what was happening. The guard quickly told him, then left running.

The wounded guard had left his rifle in the kitchen. Sid laid the fruit down and picked up the rifle. He went to the stairs and spoke.

He said, "The people now think you are crazy, Ramirez. They will be here in awhile to hang you. You have ruined too many peoples lives. I think it will take them about a half hour to get together and bring a rope. I won't let you leave as I have a rifle and will guard the stairs. You can't use the outside stairway as it is also being watched. You've done your last bit of cruelty on the people of Guadalajara. Even the police will look the other way. There is no way out for you, but suicide. So make your choice, the rope or suicide."

Sid didn't hear anything for awhile, then a shot rang out. Sid cautiously climbed the stairs and found Ramirez sitting in his chair with a hole in his head. He felt his pulse and there was none. He picked up Ramirez's gun and emptied the shells from it, then placed it where he had found it and left.

Sid saw a group of people discussing the situation. He joined the group and said, "Senor Ramirez has committed suicide. Someone needs to go get his body and place it where everyone can see it. We should have a fiesta tonight to celebrate our freedom."

The people shouted with joy. Two men placed his body in a casket sitting upright in the plaza, so everyone could view it. Many people came by and spit on his body. There was a fiesta that night and Sid took Alisa. She was dressed nicely, but he was in his white pants and shirt. They danced several dances. Near the end of the dancing, Alisa whispered, "I want you to come stay with me tonight."

Sid smiled and said, "That would be nice, but I am leaving tonight. I shall remember you though."

CHAPTER 8

BACK TO MEXICO CITY

Sid left that night and drove his buggy to Lake Chapala. He was there soon after dawn. Teresa was just getting dressed when Sid came into the room. She came into his arms and hugged him.

Sid said, "Ramirez is dead. He committed suicide. They placed his body in the plaza and most everyone came by and spat on him. They had a fiesta last night and everyone came and danced. I left soon after."

Teresa said, "I wish I could have spat on him. What will they do with his body?"

"One man told me they would put his body on the hill for the poor and will not bury it. They will leave it for the wild animals to ravish."

They went and had breakfast. As they were eating Sid

said, "Teresa, I'm leaving you here to run the clinic. I will add your name to the deed so you will be an equal partner. I have decided to go back to my sweetheart and marry her if she will have me. I hope you will be alright. With your new station in life, I'm sure you will meet someone who you can love."

Teresa said, "I knew you would leave sometime. I am much better off now, and although I knew I could never have you, I at least had you for a night or two."

"I don't regret the nights. You gave me great love. I just hope you will find someone better than me. Run the clinic and do your best."

Teresa was going to tell him she was pregnant, but decided not to trouble him. He had made up his mind. She wanted his child and it would be a comfort to her if she never found anyone. As most people new Sid's last name, they called Teresa, Doctor Porter, also, and assumed they were married.

Sid and Teresa went back to the clinic. Patients were now arriving. They didn't see Sid as he was fast asleep in his bed. Around noon he got up and packed what he needed. He took Teresa to the town hall and added her name to the deed. She wrote Teresa Porter. Sid didn't say anything as he knew the name would help her. She now had enough money coming in to live quite well.

Sid drove his buggy to Guadalajara and sold it and his horse. He then took the train to Mexico City. Arriving there the next day, he went to the post office first. There was a letter from Alta Cook. The letter had but one line that read, "Come home, I want to marry you. Love, Alta.

Sid went back to the train station and inquired about train service to Texas. There were none. He then went to a stage station and bought a ticket to Monterrey. As he traveled he could see they were building the railroad to Monterrey.

The stage took five days to reach Monterrey. It was hot and dusty. Most of the people he traveled with didn't have much to say, and that was alright with Sid. He tried to think of the many things they could do. In the end, he thought they should just get married and stay at the ranch. Let peoples tongues wag if they would, but just hold their heads high and live life to its fullest.

In Monterrey he went to Senor Ramos' ranchero. He was riding towards the hacienda when he saw Rafael Alvarado just mounting his horse. They both saw one another at the same time. Sid was off his horse and embraced Rafael and said, "When did you arrive, Rafael?"

Four days after I got your letter. I'm now married to Cloressa. Cloressa is in the house and will want to see you."

They tied their horses and went in. Cloressa immediately came into his arms. She said, "I know God sent you here. Even father believes it, now. He is very fond of Rafael and mother is happy, too. We couldn't wait for you to be here, as we didn't know where you were. Are you going back to Junction?"

Sid opened his top pocket and handed Cloressa the letter from Alta. She read it with a large smile and handed it to Rafael who then smiled. He said, "That's one way to own a ranch," and they all laughed.

Sid only spent one more day as all knew he wanted to return to Junction as fast as he could get there.

Three days later he was riding into the ranch. He could see Alta talking to two of her hands with her back to him. One of the hands recognized Sid and told her. She turned her horse and raced to him. They both hit the ground at the same time and came into each others arms then kissed.

One of the hands said to the other, "What got into those two. She laid him off and he's been gone nearly two years. I wouldn't believed it if I hadn't seen it."

The other said, "Byers, we are so dumb we could never do anything but mind cows. Sid's not like us. How the hell he worked his charm on her I don't know. She must be thirty years older than he is. However, she's prettier than any gal I've seen around here. Do you suppose they'll marry?"

"Nothing would surprise me anymore, Lenny. Like you said, we're just dumb cowboys and I like it that way."

A wedding was planned. They decided to not send invitations. They would just print an invitation in the paper that said everyone was invited. They would just let people think what they would. They were married in the Methodist Church by the new minister. He was also in the dark. He knew Alta, but he had never seen Sid. Many came out of curiosity.

After they kissed at the alter, Alta turned to the people and said, "Many of you do not know how we got together. Sid told me he has loved me since he was twelve years old. You have seen us together for ten years. He always sat by me at church and held my hand. I knew he loved me and I loved him. I was not in love with him until the year I had to let him go. He told me that he had never had another sweetheart, and that he had held only to me since he was twelve. That pierced my heart. We have written every week since he has been in Mexico. Our love grew and I decided I wanted him, and what anyone thinks is their own business. We will love each other forever."

She the turned and they kissed again. Everyone then cheered. The pastor didn't shake his head, but he wanted to.

Alta had planned a trip to New Orleans, and already had the tickets for the trip. They left on a train at four in the morning, and rode to Houston where they had to catch another train. She had timed it so they could spend the first night in a hotel.

It was after nine when they reached their hotel. They both took baths and went to eat. Although they hadn't eaten much along the way, they were still not too hungry as each was worried about sleeping with the other.

Alta had bought a special negligee with a netting cover for the honeymoon, she now had second thoughts..

They returned to their room and Alta said, "Put on your nightshirt while I change in the bathroom.

When she came out she was a picture of loveliness. Sid could not believe his eyes she was so pretty. She turned around and let him see her. She then took off the netting and was now just in the ngligee which showed all of her beautiful body. She turned around twice, then came into bed.

Sid said, "I have never seen anyone as lovely as you, Alta. You will have to help me along as you know I'm a novice at this."

Alta then pulled the top sheet down to the foot of the bed and said, "We'll just let love take its course."

They continued to New Orleans and checked into a hotel downtown. They saw the sights, but spent much of their time in their room. Sid pleased her beyond anything she ever dreamed about.

On their way home, Sid said, "How do you want to go about running the ranch, Alta?"

"I want you to be the foreman. I know everything about this ranch. I will at first tell you what I want done for the day, and you can give the crew the orders as if they were your orders. This will give the crew confidence in you. Later you will be able to see what's to be done and run it yourself. I will do what I always wanted to do, and become a housewife. Of course I will ride with you occasionally to see how the ranch is doing. We'll have fun planning for the ranch together.

It worked out that way. Six months later, Alta didn't have to tell Sid a thing and he knew what to do. Just as she had said, they had fun planning things together. The rains were good and they increased the size of their herd.

CHAPTER 9

LISA RETURNS TO THE RANCH

Just over a year and a half later, Alta's daughter, Lisa, returned to the ranch. She didn't write, she just showed up. Alta had written her about once a month, but Lisa only answered now and again.

It seems her husband was caught in bed with a neighbor's wife and was shot dead. It was too much for Lisa, so she just dropped everything after the graveside service, and came home.

Alta heard her drive up in a buggy and came out and was surprised. One of the things that came to mind was Sid. She had never told either of her daughters that she had married Sid. One good thing was that neither of her daughters knew Sid before they left.

Lisa fell into Alta's arms and said, "Frank was killed mother, and I can't return. He was caught in a neighbor's bed and was shot. I can never go back."

"What about your property, Lisa? You'll have to do something about that."

Someone else will have to deal with that, I can't face any of those people again. At the funeral, everyone shunned me, like I was responsible. I can't go back."

"Well, come in and sit down. I have some things to tell you."

They brought in all of Lisa's things and put them in her old room. They then went into the kitchen and sat. There was coffee on the stove, and Alta poured them a cup. She then said, "Lisa, I was married a year and a half ago. I didn't tell you, because I thought it would hurt you. You never came to see me, so I thought it wouldn't matter, but now that you're here, we must deal with it."

"Oh, that doesn't matter mother. Who is he?"

"It's not so much of who he is that will shock you, but that he is somewhat younger than I am."

"How much younger, Mother?"

"He's younger than you, Lisa."

"My gosh, how did you meet him mother?"

"I've known him since he was twelve years old. He told me he had loved me since the first time he ever saw me, and held only unto me from that time on. We always sat together in church and held hands when he was a boy. I loved him, but never thought of him in a romantic way until I hired him after he was grown.

"I had to let him go during the drought, because he was

the last hired. Before he left I called him up to the house to tell him goodbye. He then confessed that he was in love with me and always would be. It did something to me. My heart was pierced and we kissed goodbye. We kissed again before he left, and he told me he would write me every week, which he did.

"They were love letters and I fell in love with him. He returned a year and a half ago and we were married. Everyone in town came to our wedding. Most out of curiosity, but now everyone seems to have accepted it.

"I love him dearly, Lisa, and I always will. He runs the ranch now as good as it has ever been run. I say he runs the ranch, but we talk over every move together, and it's a pleasure for both of us. I know you will like him."

"I can't say I'm not shocked. I could never handle that with other people."

"There in lies the difference between us. I love him to where what other people think, doesn't bother me. The men he once worked with, now accept him as boss. You don't know any of them as all the old hands are gone that were here when you lived with us."

"I was just thinking, mother. Maybe your husband could go settle my business in Weatherford. He must be quite competent if he runs the ranch."

"After you are here a week or so, you may want to ask him. First get to know him and he you."

"That sounds like the way to handle it. I surely can't wait too long, as the property has to be looked after. I can give him a letter giving him authority to act for me."

"You had better see a lawyer, and have a legal paper drawn up for him to present to the authorities."

Sid came in that night and was introduced to Lisa. Sid said, "I've always wanted to know Alta's children. She means the world to me, so knowing her children is a pleasure."

Even knowing Sid was young didn't help. Lisa was shocked. He was not only younger than she was, but quite handsome. She was a little taken with him herself. She could not picture Sid and her mother in bed. A young man like that must have a large appetite for bedroom play. She still could not place her mother making love to him.

Sid was generally tired when he returned from work, because he worked right with the men. He could out do any of them, and did. They also respected him because of the medical knowledge he had treating horses and cows.

A week after Lisa arrived, they were at the dinner table when Lisa said, "Sid, I have a favor to ask you. It is not a small favor, but a large one. I had to leave Weatherford because of something my late husband did. It was so sorted that I hate to talk about it. I need for someone to go and settle my estate. Frank and I never had children, so I own everything. I need to sell out. I would ask mother, but women are not treated the same as men, so I need you to go. Will you do that for me?"

"That is a big favor. Let me talk it over with Alta tonight. We never do anything alone. We do everything together."

"Don't you ever have disagreements on what to do?"

"Yes, but after we talk it out, we always come to the same solution. Your mother is a very smart person. She ran this ranch several years before your father died, and ran it well. She taught me how to run the ranch. To me, no one is as good at running the ranch as she is. I'll let you know in the morning."

Lisa laid in bed that night thinking of her mother making love to Sid. It made her a bit jealous knowing she was receiving the pleasure that she only enjoyed for a year or so, as her husband became cold to her. She realized after his death, that he sought his pleasure with other women. She had suspected it, but would not let herself believe it. Her only pleasure was with herself.

That night they talked it over. Sid said, "It would be better if Lisa went with me. She knows all the ins and outs. I may miss something."

"I think you're right, let's try to talk to her tomorrow. With both of us, we may convince her that to get everything she has, she needs to be there."

The next morning Sid brought it up. He said, "You need to go with me, Lisa. You don't have to say a thing, unless there is something I'm missing, and that may be. It will also keep me from making a mistake that might cost you a lot of money."

"I can't bear the humiliation I will receive."

"You need to just ignore anyone who may say something. I don't think anyone will say anything with me by your side."

"People might assume you are my boyfriend, and that is why Frank did what he did."

"You can introduce me as your brother-in-law. That ought to quell any thought of that. What do you care what they think. We will just settle things, and then get out of there. Is there a hotel in Weatherford we can stay in?"

'Yes, but we could also stay at our house."

"No, I think it best that we stay in a public place."

After Alta said she knew that Sid was right, Lisa agreed to go. She didn't want to, but knew she must. She was also a little excited to be alone with a handsome man.

CHAPTER 10

THE TRIP TO AUSTIN

They left the next day. Alta said she would run the ranch as she had before. All the hands liked and respected her.

They took a buggy and traveled towards Fredericksburg, which was about sixty miles east. They traveled about thirty miles, and saw a ranch house. They had provisions for camping, but decided to ask for shelter. The rancher and his wife were named Harper. They invited them to spend the night as company was rare. Sid explained that he was Lisa's brother-in-law, so they would require separate rooms. The next day they traveled on to Fredericksburg. The hotel was meager, but did have a bath, although it was down the hall.

They left the next day for Marble Falls, and then the next day to Austin. They found a railroad had been completed to Ft. Worth which met another track to Weatherford.

They stored their horse and buggy at a livery stable in Austin and took the train. The fifth day they were in Weatherford. There was a hotel there and they had rooms next to one another. They were there by the middle of the day. Lisa had misplaced her comb and they went to a store to buy one. They entered, and as they were about to be waited on, a man was in the store and stepped near Lisa.

This man had been a friend of her husband, and he approached Lisa and said, "Is this the man you left Frank for?"

Sid took the thong off his pistol, and took a step toward the man. Sid said, "You have about five seconds to apologize to this lady, Sir, before I shoot you dead."

Sid had taken a gunfighters stance between Lisa and the man. The man knew he was about to be killed, so he reluctantly said, "I apologize, Madam, I misspoke." He then turned and walked out and went directly to the sheriff's office.

Sheriff Bob Toms had been the sheriff there for a number of years. The man explained that a stranger had just threatened his life at the general store, and he wanted him arrested for attempted murder.

Toms said, "You just stay here, Lim, I'll handle it. He left and went to the general store. Sid and Lisa were still in there when he arrived. Sheriff Toms went to the owner who was waiting on them.

Tom's said, "Harry, what did Lim say that caused this man to threaten his life."

Harry said, "He insulted the lady by asking, "Is this the man you left your husband for.'"

Tom's smiled and said, "Lim's lucky. Had it been me,

I wouldn't have given him a chance to apologize," he then turned and walked out.

Toms returned and said, "Lim, you're lucky. Had the man shot you dead, I wouldn't have even arrested him. You had better mind your tongue."

"If you won't handle this then maybe I will. Frank was my friend."

"Yes, and he was killed for sleeping with Charlie's wife, and got what he deserved. If you make further trouble, I may have to arrest you. Go on home before you land in jail or boot hill."

Lisa was thrilled with Sid's action. She already had a crush on him and this moved her crush to love. She thought, *"Frank would have just laughed off a remark like that."* She thought of Frank and was now glad he was dead.

She thought, *"Mother is way too old for Sid. I could give him the love he deserves. Oh, how I would love to be in his arms at night."*

They first went to her house. It was an upscale house with five acres. It had a barn, and a stream ran through it. There were several cows and chickens. The chickens had not been feed since Lisa had left. They had kept alive by eating worms and the spring grass.

The first thing Sid did was feed the chickens and bring the cows in. Lisa was busy cleaning the house and making something for supper. Sid milked the cows and gather the eggs. He came into a warm kitchen with a hot meal on the table. They ate and returned to the hotel.

Lisa thought of Sid that night and wondered how she could make him notice her as a woman. She thought of herself as a much more desirable woman than her mother. Sid never even thought of Lisa.

The next day they went to a land agent and asked him to sell her house. The land agent said, "You've come at an opportune time, Mrs. Lester. Property like yours is wanted by many. I will list it at a top price.

They left and went to the livery stable and asked the hostler who would be wanting to buy cows. The hostler said, "Me, for one. Let me see the boss, then I'll go with you to look them over."

Later, they were at Lisa's place, and the hostler made an offer that both Lisa and Sid thought was fair, so they left and went to the bank. The funds were transferred to Lisa's account. She then talked to the banker. She asked if he could transfer her account to the bank in Junction. She also told him she was selling her house. They made arrangements for the funds to be transferred through the Weatherford bank to the bank in Junction.

Lisa was subtle about her moves, but each chance she got to brush her body close to Sid she did. She wore her most provocative closes at night as they ate at the hotel now. The clothes were only provocative to her, but were different.

Sid did notice and decided not to mention it to her, but if it went beyond what he thought was prudent, he would explain that no one could take Alta's place.

They decided to move back to Lisa's place as they didn't know how long the sale would take, and Lisa wanted the house to stay spotless. At the house Lisa would wear her robe to breakfast and always left it open enough to show an ample amount of her breasts. She wore no slip, so at the bottom her legs showed naked past her knee. She thought eventually that Sid, being a young man, would want to explore further. However, Sid paid her no mind. This frustrated Lisa even further.

The house sold the last of the week, and funds were transferred to the bank and the bank transferred the money to Junction along with all of her other assets.

They were now on their way home. When they reached Austin, they retrieved their buggy and started out. They decided to skirt Kerrville, and cut straight across to Fredericksburg. They had to camp and Lisa saw that their bedrolls were close.

During the night a wolf howled. This was all Lisa needed to come over to Sid and say she was scared. He had not disrobed thinking that maybe she would make a move on him. When she did, she found him fully clothed, and had no chance to get her body next to his.

Sid said, "It's just a wolf, get some sleep."

She was now frustrated. She said, "Don't you want me?"

Sid just said, "No," and rolled over on his other side."

No other attempts were made by Lisa as she saw it was useless. She thought, *"That man must really love mother. Most men would have jumped my bones the first night."*

They were only twenty miles out of Junction by mid-morning. Three riders joined them. Sid was well aware of men like these, and removed the thong from his pistol. He loosened his rifle in its sleeve, also. He used his hand to reach back to his saddle bag and retrieve a box of shells. He covertly transferred the shells to an inside pocket in his vest. At noon they stopped and fixed coffee. Sid never let the men get him in a vulnerable position. However, when he took his horse to water, that was not fifty feet away, one of the men shot at him.

Sid was on the other side of the horse and the shot wounded his horse in the shoulder. Sid grabbed his rifle and canteen and hit the ground behind a deadfall. Several shots were fired, but all hit the deadfall. Sid knew he had to move, so he eased away down the deadfall that hung over the bank of the creek. He dropped down the bank and went along the edge of the creek as quickly as he could.

He knew he couldn't help Lisa as to do so would be suicide. He knew they would misuse her, but nothing he could do would help that either, unless he could get to a position to fire on them from a place they couldn't see him.

Sid worked around them, and was now on the other side of them in a cluster of rocks that was above where the men were. One of the men hollered out, "If you don't give up, we'll take your woman…. All three of us."

Sid didn't answer. To do so would give up his hiding place. He could see down into the place they had camped. He could see Lisa and a man holding her. One of the men had already taken her skirt and underwear off. He was now mounting her. She screamed, but Sid could do nothing.

One of them was taking her as the other held her. She screamed and screamed as the man did his work. They switched positions, and the other man was now taking her. Sid had a fairly good view of her and the men. Sid made sure of his aim. He didn't want to miss. He had his rifle resting on a rock, and took careful aim. He then took the slack out of the trigger just as the man pulled out of her. The bullet hit him in groin area and took away his penis and scrotum.

He screamed, then passed out. The one holding Lisa let go and grabbed his rifle.

The man not at that place yelled, "What happened, Arty?"

Her man just shot Dude's pecker off. He's bleeding like a stuck pig. I think the bullet came from those rocks west of us. While he was saying this, Sid was moving around to his previous spot, behind the deadfall on the west side.

"We're in a bad spot, Arty. We need to move."

"What about Dude?"

"If he's not dead, we'll come back for him."

"What about the woman?"

"Leave her. I'm not risking my life over some cunt."

They moved toward their horses and Sid had a clear shot in that direction as he had thought they might want out. As they reached their horse, Sid fired. It hit the man in his head and he went down like he had been hit with a sledge hammer. That left just one.

Sid yelled out, "If you mount that horse, you're a dead man. I'll let you go on foot, but I know who you are. If I ever see you in this part of the country again, I'll shoot you where you stand. So move out or die. The only reason I'm letting you alive, is that you did not mount my woman. If you had, I would have stalked you the rest of my life until I killed you."

The man left on foot going south.

Sid waited until he thought it was safe, then went to where Lisa was. He immediately started a fire as Lisa took her underwear and skirt to a stream. She then washed herself and redressed. Finally she went to the buggy for a complete change.

When she returned Sid was heating a knife to red hot. She

asked what he was doing and he said, "I'm going to cauterize that man's wounds."

"Let him die," Lisa said.

However, Sid just went on doing what he was doing. He took the red hot knife and stopped the bleeding. The man was unconscious so the pain didn't bother him. Sid put him in the back of the buggy, then retrieved the three horse. His horse was wounded, but could travel. He used one of the men's horses for their buggy, and tied the other two behind. They didn't stop when it became dark as the moon was full and the trail easy to see.

They came to town and went straight to the sheriff's office. The man in the back of the buggy had not regained consciousness. The deputy went with him to deliver the man to the doctor. While they were driving, Sid told about the men accosting them. He never said anything about the rape and Lisa was grateful.

They spent the night at the hotel and Lisa spent a long time in the bathtub. They then ate and went to bed. The next day they continued to the ranch. Sid told the story to Alta, but again left out the part about the rape. Lisa was again grateful for that.

Lisa was morose and said very little. Alta asked about that and Sid said, "She's been through a lot, Alta. She'll come around in a week or two."

Life went back to normal, but Lisa didn't. She was quiet and now read a lot. Four months passed and Lisa found she was pregnant. She told Alta, but still didn't tell her about the rape. Her stomach was now showing some. Sid didn't notice, as he was now very busy with the fall roundup.

When Alta was sure, she came to Sid and said, "I want you to leave the ranch. Go to Mexico or where ever you want, but go. I want you gone."

She was not vicious, she just was firm, and Sid could tell by her resolute face that she meant it.

Sid was shocked. He tried to reason it out in his mind, but came up with no clue. However, he knew Alta was serious, so he put together his things and left. Lisa didn't even know he was gone for two or three days, then she asked, "Where is Sid, Mother?"

"I sent him packing and you know why. If the baby wasn't due soon, I'd turn you out, too."

Lisa then realized that Alta thought Sid was the father. She said, "Oh, Mother, you've made a terrible mistake. Those men who accosted us, raped me. Had it not been for Sid all three would have taken me. Sid saved me and killed two of them. Well, one of them died later. Sid was nothing but a gentleman. You have made a terrible mistake. Oh, I wish I had told you. Sid was too much of a gentleman to tell you about the rape. Can you bring him back?"

"No, I don't know where he went. Probably to Mexico. I should have known he would not break his wedding vows. I will probably rue this day the rest of my life. Oh, what have I done? I don't blame you Lisa, I probably wouldn't have told anyone about the rape either. Oh, what have I done!"

CHAPTER 11

EL PASO AND SOUTH

Sid just thought Alta was through with him. He didn't know why, but he knew she was dead serious. Maybe she just got tired of him. With Lisa there and the baby coming on, it may have been too much for her. He never dreamed Lisa had not told Alta about the rape. That never crossed his mind.

He had heard of California and wanted to see that country. Mainly he wanted away, so he didn't hurt so much. He had seen women who got tired of their husbands. It was mostly the fault of the man not being tender, but when the wife was through with him, she never wanted him back. This generally happened when women became older. He thought this was his case. She was just tired of him, and would never want him again.

She had not wanted him sexually for sometime. He didn't

know it was caused by an infection. She wanted him just as much then as ever, but she had to get rid of the infection first. Sid didn't know this, and he took it that she was through with sex.

He had taken two horses. Both were geldings. He packed his gear on his spare horse and was well provisioned. He had withdrawn a thousand dollars from the bank in Junction before he left. He figured that was coming to him.

He joined the Pecos River near Langtry where Judge Roy Bean ruled. Sid never saw Judge Bean, but did find the river. He followed the Pecos River until it crossed the Santa Fe railroad tracks. He had been told by a prospector about the track running west to Flagstaff and then on to California. He sold his horses, saddle and most of his gear. He then boarded the train going west. He loved traveling on the railroad as he could eat in the diner and sleep in his chair.

He was in the end seat which faced another seat that contained two women in their early twenties. Both were plain, but also witty. They were headed for California also.

Sid asked, "Have you been to California before?"

"Yes, out father works for C. P. Huntington, who is one of the men who helped build the transcontinental railway."

"My that is something. Are you going to Los Angeles or San Francisco?"

"Los Angeles….. Actually near there."

They all had lively conversations for a day or so. They were traveling west of Holbrook, when the train suddenly came to a screeching halt. Sid was thrown into the girls. They were all shook up, but one of the girls giggled and said, "Are you coming on to us Sid?"

He smiled and said, "I can't help myself," which made them laugh.

They then began to hear gunfire, and raised the shade to look out. They saw many Indians attacking the train. Sid had his guns in the overhead. He strapped on his pistol and then took his rifle. As he sat down to load it, the glass windows began to be shot out.

Sid said, "Lie on the floor, girls. He then put his gun out of one of the windows and began shooting at the Indians. They weren't that easy to hit as they dodged on their horses, in and out. He did manage to shoot one Indian. Others passengers were doing the same. The Indians were now getting on the train, so he concentrated on the doors. Just as he did, one came in. He shot him dead, then the one behind him. The two blocked that door, so he turned. Just as he did, an Indian came through the passageway. Sid shot and killed the first, but the second backed off as he could see he would be shot if he entered.

Sid jumped from his chair with his pistol in hand. He went through the backdoor and saw two more Indians and shot. He missed both. They both mounted their horses and rode away. By this time several shots were being shot through the windows and many another Indian fell off his horse.

Their leader decided to pull off and they left. Sid went outside and saw a couple of the Indians still showed life, so he shot them in the head. He then went back to their car and the girls were frozen to the floor.

He said, "You can get up now, girls. The Indians have left. They both stood, but Sid could tell they were both scared. He walked up and kissed one on the cheek, then the other. Their color came back and they took their seats.

The conductor came through and said, "They derailed the engine, so we're not going anywhere. It will be morning before anyone comes to get us going again. I'll bring you some blankets as it may get cold tonight."

Sid said, "Is there anyway we can block up these broken windows to keep the wind out?"

"Come with me to the baggage car. There are cardboard boxes there, that you can wedge into the windows."

Sid and the girls followed the conductor and brought back the cardboard. They spent the next hour blocking up the windows that were broken. They then brought down their luggage and put it between the space of the two seats. With the three blanket they received by the conductor they laid them as a pad. They had two blankets and rolled the other for a pillow and the other they used as a cover.

Andrea said, "You sleep in the middle, Sid. We can then hug up to you and stay warm."

Sid said, "I like that idea," and the girls giggled. It was now getting late so they snuggled together."

Sharon said, "This is the first time Andrea that I have slept with a man."

Sid said, "Let's just hope it isn't the last time."

"You don't think they'll come back do you?"

"I've been told that the Indians don't attack at night, so we should be safe until morning."

"Andra said, "Kiss us good night, Sid." The girls were expecting a peck on the cheek, but Sid took Andra in his arms and kissed her flush on the mouth and held it for awhile. He then rolled over and kissed Sharon the same way. They were both pleased.

Andra said, "Do you think we can stay here another night?" and they all laughed."

Sharon said, "We might have to convert to the Mormon religion if we stay a week."

"Well, mother always taught us to share," and they both laughed.

Sid said, "Well, I wouldn't pick this train for our honeymoon."

Sharon said, "It looks fine to me," and they all laughed again.

Morning came and at the crack of dawn brought the Indians again. This time men in the other two cars and four in their car were ready for them and had a lot of fire power. However, the Indians had a strategy this time, and started fires under the cars.

Sid could see they would have to abandon the cars. He quickly surveyed the landscape and saw a break in the terrain about a hundred yards north from the train. He looked at the girls and said, "See if you can find some canteens or water bags. We may be here for awhile."

Sid got the last box of shells from his bag. He also had a canteen in it. The girls found a large bottle of water used in the restroom and it took both of them to carry it. As they were leaving, Sid saw a pistol and a rifle with two bandoliers full of shells by a dead man on the floor. He threw the bandoliers over his shoulder and made his way to the end of the car that was now burning rapidly. The others in their car had already left the train.

They left the train and the girls struggled as they made their way to place Sid had pointed. It was a small hill that had a steep side facing the train. There were several large rocks near the steep side. The small hill had a small indentation into its body. It created some shade and a windbreak. The rocks were large and Sid tried to push them toward the indentation. The girls came to help. It took nearly fifteen minutes to get them in place. They then piled smaller rocks on the larger ones. It made a barrier that blocked the overhang leaving them just a small opening to squeeze into.

Sid said, "I'm going back for the blankets. We'll need them tonight."

Even though their car was now nearly engulfed in flames, Sid jumped up the steps and into the burning car. He grabbed the blankets and saw a saddlebag that was full of something and took that too. As he left he could hear the battle had intensified, but knew his rifle would not be of significant help, so he traveled to the girls.

The Indians pulled off while the cars burned. Sid thought they would then rush them, thinking the people shooting at them would have no shelter.

Both girls were scared, and were glad to see Sid. He pushed in the blankets and the saddlebag. They spread the one blanket to make a pad. Sid used another blanket to cover the top of the rocks and further hide them. It was now turning dark, and the Indians had not returned.

Sid squeezed out to see what had happened. He stayed behind the small embankment and looked at the train. There were several men and women making a shelter for themselves using the floor of an unburned part of the train as the fire was now out.

The Indians had left, and he could see several braves lying on the ground. He wondered if they would come again the next day. He guessed there were twelve to fifteen men with repeating rifles. He didn't know if they had enough ammunition to carry a fight the next day. He saw several women with rifles, also, and thought this a sizable force. It was now hard to see, so he squeezed into their hiding place. The girls had a sandwich waiting for him. The saddlebag he had brought was full of food. For that he was grateful. It also contained a candle, that the girls had lit. It emitted only a small amount of light, which Sid thought was safe.

He ate the sandwich and drank some water. The girls had eaten and snuggle against him. Sharon said, "Andra, I'm in love,"

Andra said, "I am, too Sharon, I guess we will have to be Mormons," and they all laughed.

There was just room to stretch out and sleep. Sid was in the middle with the girls on both sides. They didn't wait for their kiss as both kissed him a passionate kiss.

They woke early to gunfire. The Indians were back. This time in greater numbers, as they had gathered another tribe to aid them. The people from the train were lead by a cavalry officer who knew the art of defense. He had made a fort out of one of the cars and covered all sides. The Indians could not penetrate it. The men and some of the women were crack shots, and could pick an Indian off at a hundred yards. They were prudent with their shots, and most of the time brought down an Indian with every shot.

The Indians decided to make a charge with all their force and overwhelmed the fort. It worked to a certain extent, but the Indians lost a lot of men doing it. Fighting began man to man. The women shot their pistols. It looked like a draw.

Only a few whites were left and only a handful of Indians. The Indians pulled away leaving a mass of dead bodies. The whites had two men and three women. both men were wounded and one of the women was shot through the shoulder.

As they were tending to their wounds, just over ten Indians charged their position. Another fight ensued and all the whites were killed. Only two Indians remained.

The Indians were about to take scalps when Sid's rifle rang out and one of the Indians clutched his chest. The other could see Sid standing not a hundred feet from him. The Indian was out of ammunition and just yelled and charged him with his knife.

Sid let him come within twenty-five feet of him then pumped two bullets into him that dropped him in his tracks. He walked up and could see the hate in the Indians eyes. Sid smiled at him and said, "You should have left well enough alone. Whites always win."

The Indian understood English, and in his heart had to agree as he passed onto the happy hunting ground.

Sid yelled, "It's over, girls. You can come out now."

There was no way to bury the people. Sid said, "We have to leave here. We'll make up packs and walk west on the tracks. They made up packs and bedrolls and by noon were walking away. They didn't look back.

Sid wondered why no relief train had come. They walked

on and at dusk made camp by a stream under a trestle. Sid made a fire and they had a coffee pot, but no coffee. Sid shaved some jerky in the water and let it boil awhile. He then poured the girls some broth. They were happy to have something warm, as it had turned cold. They found a place under the trestle that gave them a break from the north wind. They again huddled up and slept.

Come morning, Sid heated the broth and they each had a cup and then packed up and walked on. They were all tired. The girls especially, as they were not used to walking.

At mid afternoon, they saw another wooden trestle that had been burned. Men were working on it and a train sat on the other side of the trestle. They traversed the stream that the trestle spanned at one time, and went to the last car that was a special car for an executive of the railroad. The executive recognized the two girls as daughters of a man who assisted C. P. Huntington. He gave them royal treatment. He welcomed them in and they spent the next few minutes telling what happened.

The executive was Cole Carter, the superintendent for that area. He ordered the train to take them to Flagstaff, as he needed more men, also.

At Flagstaff, they went to a hotel and all had a hot bath. It was now dark and they were all starved. Although they were ragged, they went to the hotel dining room and had a bottle of wine with their steaks. The wine had taken its toll, and they were all very tired.

Sid had just got into bed when the two girls entered his room and got on each side of him. Andra said, "A girl can't sleep without her husband."

Sid didn't argue, he was too tired. They were all asleep in minutes. The next morning was spent buying clothes. The girls charged all the clothes, including Sid's to their father. All the merchants had been told by Cole to just charge it to the railroad. Sid had decided to go back to El Paso. He still thought of Alta. He could still see her face as she told him to get out. He thought that she had just changed. He had seen older people while he grew up, get tired of one another. He thought maybe Alta was just tired of him. This made him want to see Mexico where he had friends.

A few days later they received word that the trestle that had been burned had been repaired. Sid knew a train was coming through going east, so he decided to tell the girls. He told them at breakfast that morning that he was married. He said, "I wasn't stringing you along, I just didn't want to spoil your fun."

They had long faces, so he said, "Someday I may visit to you in Los Angles, but the time isn't now. I need to go home."

They saw him off and both kissed him a passionate kiss goodbye. Once on the train Sid was talking with a Mexican man. The man was telling him that a railroad now ran south from El Paso to Terreon and they were building the tracks south from their to Mexico City.

Sid was glad to hear that. The trip to Mexico City was a thousand miles or more, but by train he could sleep and eat comfortably. His ticket to El Paso was given to him by the railroad to compensate him for his discomfort.

The trip from El Paso, south, went well. It was not as comfortable as the train to El Paso, as the dining car was much poorer. However, he enjoyed the trip. When they reach

Chihuahua City, several Mexican men boarded the train. They were men from the revolution. They began robbing the people. One of the men came to Sid and said, "Get up gringo and come with me."

Sid was taken to the leader of the rebels. His name was Poncho Villa. He said, "I will hold you for ransom."

Sid didn't say anything as to do so may cause the man to have him shot. A woman came in bringing wine for Poncho. He said, "Juanita, put this gringo in the room next to yours, and bring him something to eat."

Sid walked with her to the room. Sid asked, "Are you Villa's woman?"

"Yes, but I hate the pig. He uses me like a whore. I have no say in the matter. I even thought about killing myself."

"Well, don't do that. I want to escape and I will take you with me. You can pose as my wife and we can disguise ourselves as older people."

"That may work, but not tonight. They will watch you tonight. After three or four days they don't watch you so close."

"Do you have a family?"

"No, my husband was killed by those pigs, and Poncho took me as his woman. He had another woman, but just passed her off to one of his men, as he thought I was more comely."

"You are pretty. I can see why he took you. I'm married, so you'll have no trouble with me. I just want to get out of Chihuahua City. Do you know where we can go?"

"The train and road to El Paso will be watched as will the road to Terreon. I have an uncle and aunt in San Juanito that is about sixty kilometers southwest of here. The trail is difficult, but there is also water along the way. I have traveled that way several times. There are numerous places to hide along the way when the mountains start. If we can travel about eight kilometers without being seen, I can hide us, then, and they will never find us.

"We will need food, a canteen, a bedroll and some old clothes. I will see to that. I suggest that we leave about midnight two days from now. I can bring your guards a bottle of mescal and they will be asleep by midnight. Then we go.

"If they think you won't bring them ransom money they will shoot you. I've seen it before. Tell Poncho a story of a rich father that will pay ransom."

Just as Juanita said, the next morning Poncho brought him in and asked who could ransom him?"

Sid said, "I am married to the daughter of an executive with C. P. Huntington, the man who owns many railroads. If you write to Mr. Huntington, he will provide what you ask, as he likes me. As a matter of fact, I am on an errand for Mr. Huntington, to see how the railroad is coming below Terreon. Mr. Huntington has money tied up in it."

Poncho said, "I want you to write out the letter. I will provide you with stationary from the general. That will impress Mr. Huntington as he knows we mean business. How much do you think Mr. Huntington will pay for you?"

"I would say two thousand dollars. If you go too high, he will just write me off as a bad investment."

This made Poncho laugh. "He said, "I believe you, now. I wouldn't pay more than two hundred for my son-in-law," and laughed again. He then turned and said, "Juanita, bring us some wine. I like this man. I may let you sleep with Juanita tonight. I have to go to Terreon. Take care of him Juanita. I want a good report when I return."

Juanita smiled, but Sid knew this was just for show. She came to Sid that night and said, "The time to go is tonight. With Poncho gone, the men will be more relaxed. I have assembled what we need. Be ready to go at midnight."

Sid was ready to go when Juanita came with the clothes and gear they needed. She said, "The guards are asleep, let's go."

Sid slipped into the clothes she brought him and put on the sombrero she handed him. He put on his backpack with the bedroll tied at the top. They walked out and Juanita took them down a back street that led to the trail they would follow. She walked fast as the moon was full and was bright. They walked until mid-day when hills began to abut the trail. By two that afternoon, she went off the trail, and led them south for about a kilometer. There she ascended a large hill that was covered with brush and cacti. She led him to a cave. They went inside and Sid could see it was a deep cave.

Juanita lit a candle and they went about a hundred feet into the cave. Sid could hear water dripping and saw a small pool. He was very thirsty and went to his belly and drank the cool water.

They laid out their bedrolls, and Juanita brought out some tortilla's with goat meat. Sid was famished and ate all she gave him. They then laid down and slept. Sid did not know how long they slept, but rose when Juanita said, "It's time to go."

She already had two candles lit and Sid rolled up his bedroll and tied it to the top of his backpack, and they left. The same moon was above and they went back to the trail they had followed. Juanita knew the small trail. They were soon back to the main trail and on their way. They reached San Juanito at dusk and Juanita took Sid to her uncle's house. It was an adobe with three rooms.

Juanita introduced Sid as her new husband. She explained that her husband had been killed by the rebels. The uncle and aunt appeared hospitable and her aunt fixed them something to eat. It was bean stew with some goat meat and peppers in it. It was nearly too hot for Sid to eat, but he washed it down with some water.

They were then shown to the bed they would sleep on. When they were in bed, Juanita said, "I knew they had but one bed. If they thought you were a fugitive, they would turn you in. I don't trust them. I have heard stories about them before. Sid rolled over and went to sleep.

He still had a considerable amount of money on him as he had a hidden pocket in his other clothes that he had brought along.

The next morning, Sid told Juanita that he needed to get a map so he could make plans to get away. Sid changed into his other clothes and hat, and Juanita showed him a store that sold maps. They bought a map then went to a place to have breakfast. As they were eating, Sid studied the map and saw if they could travel south some thirty kilometers, they could reach a river that would take them to Los Mochas. It was on the coast. From there they may be able to catch a boat to Porto Vallarta, which was west from Guadalajara.

He looked at Juanita and said, I will take you along if you want to go. As I told you before, I'm married, so you could not be my woman even if you wanted me."

"I have no where to go. Maybe I can start a new life in Guadalajara."

They didn't even go back for their things as Juanita thought it wise to just depart. Her aunt had seen Sid in his American clothes. Juanita was right, as the aunt had gone to the authorities to see if there was any reward on the gringo. There wasn't, so she returned and went through their packs and bedrolls, but found nothing.

They asked and found a man who would take them in his buggy to a port on the river. He said, "There are barges that go to Los Mochas. For a few pesos they will take you along."

It worked out well and they reached Los Mochas the next day. The first thing Sid did was to buy Juanita new underwear and a new outfit. Sid also bought some nice Mexican clothes and a suitcase. They carried the clothes to a bathhouse and bathed. The bathhouse had a barber who shaved and cut Sid's hair then worked on Juanita's hair until she looked nice. They then went to inquire about a ship. They found that a passenger ship docked once a week, so they had two days to kill before it arrived.

They went to a hotel and checked in as man and wife. Sid asked for two beds, but there was none available, so they took one with a double bed. They spent their day looking at the map and making plans.

That night Juanita put on her nightshirt as did Sid and went to bed. Not long after they went to bed Juanita raised her nightshirt and put her body onto the back of Sid. Although he wanted her, be bore up to the fact that she may become pregnant.

"The next morning Juanita said, "You must love your wife very much to resist the temptation."

Sid said nothing. The next day the ship arrived and they boarded. They had several stops along the way, but finally arrived at Porto Vallarta. They found that a stage ran to Guadalajara.

CHAPTER 12

A TRIP POSTPONED

Sid asked about the rebels and if the stage would be safe. The clerk said, "We have had some trouble, but that was some months ago. You and your wife should be safe."

Juanita said, "I like it when people refer to me as your wife. I feel like I am your wife minus the sex. Will we stay together in Guadalajara?"

"Yes, until I can get you situated."

"Do you have any skills, Sid."

"Yes, I'm a doctor for animals. I also have been a doctor for people at a prison for a year. At Lake Chapala, I had a clinic that I turned over to my nurse when I returned to my wife."

"Tell me about your wife."

"Sid said, "To begin with, she's thirty years older than me."

"How could you love someone that old?"

"I fell in love with her when I was twelve and never loved anyone else. I strayed once, but only because the woman need me, as she was terribly scared. That was the only way I could calm her."

"That is good to know. Tonight I may become very frightened."

Sid laughed and said, "You're a delight to be with, Juanita. In different circumstances, I could see us together. However, I'm not ready now. I have to lose the pain that's inside me."

The first day went well. They stayed at a way station that night. They were off early and traveled until noon. They came to a small village and stopped for lunch. They were off again and traveled about an hour, then the coach came to a stop. They were surrounded by Mexican rebels.

They were ordered to get out of the coach. They took the strong box and robbed all that were in the coach. Sid had most of his money in a secret pocket and just gave the rebels what was in his wallet. Juanita always wore the gold wedding band that was given to her by her late husband. She clung to Sid as she was scared.

The leader said, "You gringo, your wife and you will stay with us. The rest can continue." As soon as the passengers were loaded the stage left with Sid and Juanita standing there.

The leader was Carlos Mendez. He was near forty and it was obvious that he was the leader, as he rode a fine stallion, and his saddle and clothes were much better than the others. Carlos said, "So why are you traveling to Guadalajara, Gringo?"

"We were captured by Poncho Villa's men and they took my wife and misused her. One of them had a venereal disease and transmitted it to my wife. We escaped and were trying to get back to Guadalajara so we could get the medicine to cure her."

"What do you know about medicine, Gringo?"

"I'm a doctor."

"We need a doctor as some of my men were shot in our last raid. We will take you to our headquarters in San Marcos. We need you to extract the bullets in some of my men, and doctor the others."

"Do you have the tools and medicine I will need to extract the bullets?"

"We don't, but I will send for the medicine the tools you need. You must make a list of everything you will need. I will send someone to Guadalajara for them right now."

They were taken to San Marcos and it was late when they arrived. They were put in a room with one bed. No one guarded them, but they knew it was impossible to escape.

When they were alone, Juanita said, "That was smart of you to tell them I had a venereal disease. No one will touch me now. However, we are together in one bed and I was scared, and there is only one way to calm me down."

Sid didn't answer, he just pulled off his clothes, and washed up with soap, as an ewer and wash basin were in their room. After he had washed, Juanita washed, also, and by the time she reached the bed, Sid was asleep.

The next day was spent looking at the rebels who had been shot. He asked Mendez to clean out a hall that had been used for assembles by the people of San Marcos. It was cleaned thoroughly and beds with clean linens were brought in. Sid had the wounded bathed in a bathhouse and put on clean white pants and shirts. Sid then looked at the ones who had bullets still in them. He had a table that had a clean sheet on it. When the tools and medicine arrived, Sid examined the wounds then operated.

Sid took them one at a time and Juanita worked as his nurse. He was able to extract all the bullets in the men by six that evening. He was dead tired. Juanita was helpful as she boiled water and cleaned wounds then wrapped them, after antiseptic was applied. Two men died during the night.

Mendez was impressed. He said, "You are now part of the revolution. You have performed a valuable service for us and I will pay you well."

However, the very next morning federal forces attacked them. Mendez and just a few of his troops escaped. The captain of the Federalies asked Sid, "Why are you helping the rebels."

Sid said, "We were on a stagecoach headed for Guadalajara when Mendez captured us. He had wounded men, and I'm a doctor, so I tried to keep them alive. Unfortunately several died of their wounds."

"I ought to arrest you for aiding the enemy, but I see you were just administering kindness. Many others would have had you shot, you know."

"Yes, many minds are skewed in the governing and revolution."

"I will see you get on your way to Guadalajara," which he did. He acquired a two wheeled buggy and horse for them. That afternoon they rode away with an escort of four men. At dusk that night they were attacked by Mendez. The four man escort was killed, but they drove Mendez away. Only Mendez and one man, who was wounded, rode away.

Sid turned to say something to Juanita, but she had a bullet hole through her head. Sid was very sad. He had no shovel, so he left, but wrapped Juanita in a blanket and put her in the back of his buggy and rode away. He came to a farm and the farmer and his sons helped bury Juanita. After that was done, Sid was asked to spend the night. The farmer was well to do, and treated him nicely.

The next morning the farmer was showing Sid his barn and a cow that had eaten some loco weed. Sid knew just what to do, and doctored the cow. The farmer was elated and asked him to stay for a few days. He also had two daughters who he wanted Sid to meet. They were plain and very quiet. Sid just nodded to them. After another day, Sid was on his way.

He stopped in a village not far from Guadalajara and decided to have something to eat at the local cantina. He entered and was eating when Mendez came in. He saw Sid and came right over and sat with him.

Mendez laughed and said, Doctor Porter, our lives seemed to cross quite often. I think it's karma."

Mendez ordered and bought a bottle of wine for them both. He was personable and Sid liked him.

Sid said, "How did you get mixed up in this revolution, Mendez. You look like an intelligent man."

"I was broke and thought I could profit by it. I'm not a fool. There will always be revolutions in Mexico, because the people are treated badly, no matter who is in power. However, after the shooting is over, the rebels become just like the men they were fighting. I know that. However, I can rob legally because I am doing so for a cause. My cause is to siphon off enough of the profits from our raids, so I may become rich.

I am well on my way. Why don't you come with me, I will make you rich while having a good time."

"Sounds interesting, but I need to get back to my medical practice. I worked for a doctor in Guadalajara and hopefully he will employ me again. Helping people is something I must do. I think it is a gift from God."

Mendez crossed himself and said, "I too, believe in helping people." He then grinned and said, "I also help myself. I count you as a good friend, doctor, and hopefully we will meet again. I get into Guadalajara several times each year, so I will see you."

* * *

Doctor Contreras was glad to see Sid. He said, "I have too many patients. You couldn't have come at a better time. I was just thinking this morning '*If only Doctor Porter were here,*' and you just popped in. The Lord must have heard me and brought you here. You will not be doctoring animals, as my case load with people has increased dramatically. I will give you the people who are not in too bad of shape."

Sid smiled and said, "If you only knew what it took to get me here, you would be amazed. I will tell you about it when we are less busy."

Sid jumped right into the work. He learned more everyday from Dr. Contreras. The doctor said, "You will be better than I am in a year or two. You have a natural talent for surgery, and your nimble hands tie sutures better than I can." The doctor had medical books that he wanted Sid to read.

He said, "Sid, medicine is changing by the day. New

procedures are being used that I never heard about. I have acquired many books from America, but am not that versed in English. Please read these books every chance you get, and then you can relate them to me. I am fascinated with these new discoveries, and I am sure you will be."

Much of Sid's off time was now spent reading the journals. He enjoyed going over some of the procedures with Dr. Contreras.

* * *

The President of Mexico was now Benito Juarez. He had a general who was loyal to him, but also stole from the people. His name was Carlos Diaz. He hated people who opposed President Juarez. He was brutal with rebels, often torturing them and shooting them. He was a demanding man who lived an opulent life style.

Sid was eating in a restaurant one night, and Mendez suddenly appeared and took a seat at his table. Sid was pleased to see him and they had dinner, together.

Mendez said, "I have made myself invisible for the past year, as Diaz is very brutal. They know who I am, but I am very careful not to be seen often. No one bothers me, as they are afraid if they try to take me, many of my followers will do them in.

"It was just by chance I saw you enter the restaurant. I saw a chance to have dinner with you, my friend."

Each told what they had been doing, and had a nice time drinking wine and talking. Mendez said, "I like President Juarez. He's a fair man, who is for the people. Unfortunately, he has General Diaz with him. Diaz is a butcher. Beware of him."

Unbeknown to them, one of Diaz's men was at the restaurant eating and knew Mendez by sight. He also knew of the doctor. The next day he reported to Diaz about Mendez being in Guadalajara.

Diaz said, "I would like to catch that scoundrel, but too many people think of him as a hero and would come to his aid."

The man reporting said, "He was having dinner with the doctor who his helping Doctor Contreras. I believe his name is Doctor Porter."

"Pick the doctor up," Diaz ordered. "I want to interview him and find out his connection with Mendez. Tell him that I just want to talk with him, and be courteous."

The next day at his office, a soldier came and asked Sid if he would come with him. He said, "The general has heard about your work, and wants to talk with you."

Sid went with him to the generals headquarters that was in an elaborate building built by Maximilian.

It was near lunch time and Diaz had timed it so he could ask Sid to have lunch with him, which Sid did. Sid could tell that Diaz lived an opulent lifestyle. He ordered his servants around like they were slaves. One woman was so nervous that she spilled the wine on the table clothe. Diaz stood and slapped her and tore her dress in the process.

Diaz was very pleasant to Sid, and asked him if he would come back that night. He said they were having a fiesta and a traveling show would be on hand.

Sid agreed, and that night as he was being shown in, he

saw the woman who Diaz had slapped and tore her dress. She took Sid's hat and Sid caught her hand as she was taking his hat and covertly put fifty pesos in her hand. She had no idea how much he gave her, but she gave him a nice smile and said, "Thank you, Doctor."

The show didn't start until late, and lasted a long time. Sid really enjoyed the show. Diaz said, "Doctor, I would like you to spend the night. I have some things I want to talk over with you in the morning."

As it was late, Sid agreed and was put in nice room. Sid was asleep when a woman woke him. She had her finger over her lips. She whispered, "They are going to shoot you in the morning. I overheard Diaz give the order. Come with me."

Sid gathered up his shoes and clothes and followed her in his night shirt. As there were guards on every outside door, Sid was in a quandary of where he was to go. The woman led him into a secret panel that she was able to move as if by magic. They stepped into a narrow hallway lit by candlelight. Sid followed her to a secret room.

When they arrived another woman was there. She said, "This mansion has many secret hallways and rooms that Diaz knows nothing about. We have a secret listening place so we can hear every word that Diaz says. He ordered his men to shoot you in the morning. We know you heal our people, and are a friend of Carlos Mendez. We will hide you until we can reach Mendez, then he will take you to safety."

There was a bed in the room and the woman said, "You will sleep here. I will sleep with you."

She had said it like it was a command, so Sid said nothing. Sid was still in his night shirt and was carrying his clothes.

He climbed into bed and the woman blew out the lamp. She stayed on her side of the bed and in moment was breathing easy, while Sid laid awake. Finally he fell asleep. He was wakened by screaming and shouting. Sid could hear the loud voice. It was Diaz. He shouted, "How did he leave here. Have the guards report to my office. I want to know who let him out. Some of you must be loyal to that pig, Mendez!"

Sid was given some brown mush with brown sugar on it. He ate in silence at a table. The woman he had slept with was gone and a young woman was there.

Sid said, "Who was the woman I slept with last night?"

The girl laughed and said, "That was my mother, Maria. She treated you as if you were her little boy." This made Sid smile as he looked at the girl. She was a beauty.

She continued, "We know Mendez is your friend. He is a hero to our people. He is very good to us. He keeps the soldiers in line as they fear him, as they know we are behind him."

"Will I be here another night?"

"That I cannot say, as Mendez must be found."

"Will your mother and you take turns sleeping with me?"

The girl laughed and said, "My mother would kill us both."

"What does your mother do here?"

"She runs this place. She sees to everything and the General likes her. He does not know how she hates him."

"Why doesn't she have the cook poison him."

"I never thought of that. I will suggest it to mother. However, mother is very religious and I don't see her condoning murder."

"Are you religious like your mother?"

"Yes, but I could poison Diaz and not lose a wink of sleep."

"I'll be careful not to make you mad at me," and she smiled.

Mendez came in the middle of the night. Maria had given the guards at one door a quart of mescal, so they were fast asleep at their posts. Mendez had horses and they traveled until daylight, then pulled into a small village. He rode to an adobe hut and said, "You stay here. I have things I must do."

Sid entered the adobe and was met by a middle aged woman. She smiled and asked, "Are you hungry?"

Sid nodded and she said, "I am Consuella Ortiz. Carlos is my cousin."

Consuella began cooking eggs. She made an omelet that had cheese, beans, peppers and onions in it. It was very tasty and Sid told her so. After eating, the woman showed Sid a bed as she could tell he was tired. Sid started to just lie down, but the women helped him off with his clothes and gave him a night shirt.

He woke that afternoon. She had an outhouse and when Sid returned from it, he could smell food cooking. She had a stew and it was delicious. She ate with Sid and she often looked at him. He would then smile at her.

Consuella said, "Carlos has a surprise for General Diaz. You are to stay here until that happens."

"What is the surprise?"

"Diaz has been looking for you. He has many men scattered out looking in every casa. Carlos has laid clues to lead him here. Diaz will have about fifty soldiers with him. He will be with them as he wants to hang you publicly, now that you have escaped from him. He will arrive tomorrow morning, probably near noon."

Sid enjoyed Consuella and they talked of Mexico and where it was heading. She believed that if Juarez could weed out people like Diaz, then Mexico may have a chance.

Just as she had predicted, Diaz came to her adobe before noon the next day. He shouted, "Doctor Porter, you are a traitor to Mexico. I am here to hang you!"

A rope was then thrown over a limb of a tree about fifteen feet off the ground. Sid stepped out as he didn't want Consuella hurt. She stayed back in the shadows where she could see everything, but not be seen by Diaz.

Sid said, "How have I been a traitor to Mexico, General Diaz?"

"You aided the rebels by tending their wounds."

"That's the job of a doctor."

"Then you admit helping the enemy."

"They were not the enemy to me, just wounded men. I'm an American Citizen and have no stake in the revolution. If you hang me, my friends in America will go to our president and he will ask President Juarez to give you up to America for murdering one of its citizens."

Diaz said, "I don't care about your government. It means nothing to me. I hereby sentence you to death by hanging."

A voice then rang out. "How are you going to do that?"

Diaz looked around and there were over two hundred men with rifles pointed at the fifty soldiers and Diaz. He was stunned.

Mendez said, "Your soldiers have but one choice. Hang Diaz or die right here."

The soldiers started muttering among themselves. One of the soldiers who was near Diaz jumped to him, and took him off his horse to the ground. Several others then used rope and bound his hands behind his back, then brought him to his feet. They marched him over to the tree where someone had provided a chair. They put the rope around his neck and brought the rope taunt.

Mendez said, "Do you have any last words, Diaz?"

"If you will spare my life, I will make you all rich. I have hidden vast amounts of treasure near here. I will lead you to it, if you will spare me."

"Sounds very good," said Mendez. "Take the rope off of him."

Diaz let out a sigh and said, "Bring my horse."

Mendez said to the soldiers, "You are now rebels as by your actions you have fought against the government. Leave your rifles and go."

The soldiers shed their rifles and rode away.

Diaz took Mendez to the place of his treasure. It was in a draw that led to a cave in the mountain. There, they unearthed a vast treasure of gold, silver, ammunition and guns. They sent for wagons and hauled all of it away.

While they were waiting for the wagons to arrive Mendez said, "You are free to ride away, Diaz, however, your men now know what you've done. If I were you, I would leave Mexico before Juarez finds out you have stolen from the people."

Diaz thought, *I will go to Juarez and tell him my version of this, before the word comes to him about the treasure.* He rode back to the village and saw some of his soldiers. He tried to order them to help him, but they shunned him saying, "You are a traitor, and we won't help you. Word is now been given to your troops on what you have done. They will hang you soon enough."

Back where the treasure was being loaded, Mendez said, "I will give each man two hundred pesos for helping me bring down Diaz. I will take the rest for the revolution."

Sid was thinking, "*The revolution is his personal treasure.*"

Diaz was not riding toward Guadalajara. He caught the train from there to Mexico City. He went to the palace and asked to see President Juarez.

He told Juarez what had transpired. Dias said, "The treasure was for making Mexico strong under your leadership, Excellency. When I needed money to pay our army I used that treasury. Now it is the hands of that traitor, Mendez." He didn't mention Sid. He only referred to him as "the traitor." He also told Juarez that there would be people coming to discredit him, but not to believe them, because Mendez was sending them as they worked for the new revolution.

Juarez knew that Diaz had fought gallantly in the revolution. He did not always think Diaz's methods were right, but the results were good. He reassigned him to Monterrey, as the commander there had resigned because of sickness.

CHAPTER 13

A MESSAGE FROM HOME

When Sid reached Guadalajara, he decided to see if there were any mail for him. There was a letter, and it was from Lisa. She said that Alta was low and may not live. The doctor said she had cancer.

Sid left immediately. He took the train to Mexico City and found there was another train to Monterrey. He reached Monterey before noon the next day. He went directly to a livery stable and bought a horse. He bought supplies and a bedroll and was off. He rode due north for four days and crossed the Rio Grande River at Del Rio. He then went northeast toward Junction.

He knew most of this country and was able to find the streams and watering holes. It had been ten days since he had left Guadalajara, when he rode up to the ranch house.

Lisa met him on the front porch and said, "I'm sorry, Sid, Mother passed away yesterday. Her last words were for you. She said, 'Tell him I loved him,' then passed on."

Sid was expecting it, but it was still a heavy blow. He went into the house and there was a casket. Lisa raised the lid and Sid looked at Alta. She was beautiful. She looked just like she was sleeping. She was much thinner than Sid remembered her.

Lisa left and Sid stood for better than a half hour viewing her and remembering the times they spent together.

They buried her the next day. Lisa had his arm. Laura, Alta's other daughter, was there. The minister who had married Alta and Sid did the service and then prayed. When they returned to the house, Lisa said, "When mom sent you away, she thought that my baby was yours. I didn't realize that for two days after you left. I then told her the baby was from the rape. She then realized she had made the worse mistake of her life. She told me how much she loved you, and should have known you would never have done that. How tragic. I feel responsible. I just took it for granted that she knew it was those men who raped me. I then realized that neither of us had told her about the rape as it was a sensitive thing to talk about.

She left you everything that belonged to her. I even encouraged her to leave the ranch to you."

"No Lisa, the ranch should go to Laura and you. I'm going back to Mexico. I have nothing left in Texas and I do in Mexico."

"What do you have in Mexico, Sid?"

"I practice medicine in Guadalajara. I want to leave here as there are so many memories of Alta. I'll have the bank transfer the property and her savings to you and Laura before I leave."

When they were alone, Lisa said, "I think we could make a life together, Sid. Would you give it a try?"

Sid smiled and said, "I thank you, Lisa, but you're too old for me." This brought a smile from Lisa. Sid then said, "It would be no good, Lisa. You may have feelings for me, but it would just go against the grain with me as I loved only your mother. I would always think of her and that would be no good for either of us."

Lisa understood that Sid didn't love her, so she said no more.

Two days later, after all the business had been was finished, Sid packed up and left. He took two horses that were very good. He had geared up well.

Lisa said, "Will you write once in awhile?"

Sid said, "Maybe. I won't promise."

"Let me hug you before you go, Sid. If you ever get lonely for Texas, I'll be here for you. I now see what mother saw in you."

When Sid arrived in Monterrey he went directly to the Alvarodo hacienda. They were all glad to see him, He was told that Rafael now ran the ranch for Estonia Romero, Cloressa's father. Tina had married and was living in Vera Cruz.

Sid spent the night, but was off to see Rafael and Claressa the next morning.

He was greeted warmly by Rafael and all the Romero family. He stayed two days with them, but was now anxious to get back to Guadalajara.

Sid reached Mexico City, and after bathing and having a

shave and a haircut, he saw a poster that had Rico's picture on it. Rico was now staring in a show at the best nightclub in the City. Sid bought a ticket from a man trying to sell his ticket as the show was sold out. He had to pay a premium price for the ticket, but he thought it worth it. The show was tremendous and Rico was outstanding. The crowd gave them a standing ovation and clapped until Rico came out and sang another song. He was accompanied by two women who had beautiful voices that blended perfectly with Rico's voice. They again stood to a standing ovation and the crowd wanted more, but Rico just bowed and pointed to the two women who the crowd clapped thunderously for.

Sid waited until the crowd started to thin, then went to the stage and told one of the guards that he was a personal friend of Rico and his sister. The guard had loved Rico's sister and hung his head and said, "I still cry when someone mentions her name. I loved her. She died too early. Did you know her?"

Sid said, "I was staying at her house when she died. People came until well after dark. It was a sad thing, especially for Rico. He loved her more than any of us."

The guard was weeping now and motioned Sid in.

Rico was ecstatic when he saw Sid. He still had most of his makeup on, but he burst in next door where the women were undressing and said, Salentra! The man I was telling you about, is here! She came forward half undressed, but came to where Rico was. She said, "He's much better looking than what you described., Rico. Welcome to Mexico City, Dr. Porter.

Sid was amazed that she knew him by name. Salentra said,

"leave us now. We want to get out of here. Rico is taking us to a party.

Sid waited until Rico had all his makeup off and changed into a handsome suit. They went to the door where the women were, and Rico just opened the door and they went in. Other girls were there and some were near naked, but they paid them no mind as if it were a common occurrence.

They left and two more girls came with them. There names were Landra and Quenta. Sid had never heard those names before. Quenta and Salentra each took one of Sid's arms while the other two took Rico's arms. They went to a special dining room that was upstairs. It was exclusive. The headwaiter met them and took them to a special room where a three string trio was playing classical music. They stopped when Rico and his party arrived and made deep bows.

Rico said in a voice where the musicians could hear and said, "I should be bowing to those men, they are the real musicians. The three smiled, and continued playing. The table was set with a linen tablecloth with sterling silverware and beautiful china.

Rico said, "I have some bad news for you girls. Dr. Porter is married."

Sid said, "I lost my wife four weeks ago to cancer, Rico. I got there a day late. I was there to put her in the ground though. They told me she was sick for a year, so it was a blessing when she passed. I had been in love with her since I was twelve, so it is a great loss. I know I must start anew, but it will be hard. Maybe you girls and Rico can get me out of the gloom I'm in."

Salendra said, "I'll do my best," and the other girls and

130

Rico laughed. The wine steward was there, and Rico knew just what they needed. He ordered Champaign. It was from France, and was better than good. It had been chilled to the perfect temperature. Sid never liked Champaign, but he liked this one. They all took a sip and Salendra said, I will start the party by kissing Dr. Porter."

Tico said, "She always wants dessert first," and they all laughed as Salendra took Sid in her arms and kissed him.

The party was great. All the girls had marvelous senses of humor, and kept Sid laughing. Rico was the best.

Sid asked, "Are any of you girls married?"

Quenta said, "We all have been married, but they didn't like us sleeping with Rico and left us. Can you image how selfish some men are," and they all laughed.

Tico said, "To know Rico, is to sleep with him," and they all laughed again.

Sid said, "Does he have any favorites?"

"Yes, Salendra said, "The one he is with that night," and they all laughed again.

"I will say this," Landra said, "He's true to us four."

Tico said, "He better be, or I'll brain him and call him a womanizer," and they all laughed again.

Rico began telling jokes and Sid laughed until his sides hurt. After a splendid meal, Rico said, "Let's all go to my place. It's getting late, and I have to be up by noon."

Sid had not checked into a hotel. He had all his gear at the livery stable. Rico had a coach and they dropped by the stable and picked up his things. By this time everyone called him, Sid."

Landra asked, "Where are you from, Sid?"

"I'm originally from Texas, but I have lived in Mexico for a few years, and now call Guadalajara my home. I practice there with another doctor."

"I thought you said you were married to a women in Texas."

"She threw me out a few years ago, as she thought I had slept with her daughter. However, she learned later that her daughter had been raped, and was so embarrassed about it she didn't tell my wife until I was gone. We both suffered from that. We did have about two years together that were the happiest two years of my life."

"She was very young to have cancer, Tico said, "That generally comes after you are older."

She was thirty years older than me, but the time gap made no difference to me. It did to her, until we kissed, then she loved me dearly, until the misunderstanding occurred."

"Thirty years," said, Landra, "Then I still have a chance," and the girls exploded in laughter. Landra was the oldest at thirty-two.

Queta said, "I think we should share him, unless Rico objects."

Rico said, "By all means, I can't keep up with any two of you," which brought more laughter.

"Yes, I can see now we need to bring in some new blood to our arrangement," said Tico. "In a few years we will have to put Rico out to pasture, then where would we be."

"I'm not that old," said Rico.

They had a few more drinks and then Sid said, "I have to go to bed. I've been up nearly twenty hours and with the liquor I have consumed, I would be no good to anyone."

The girls said, "Aah." Then Tico said, "Rest up big boy, your harem is waiting," and they all laughed.

Sid woke the next morning around eight, and the house was completely silent. He went into the kitchen and made some coffee. He left and bought a paper then dropped by a bakery, and brought back a dozen sweet rolls. He read the paper and read an article praising Rico and his troupes performances. There was also an article that said the revolution had ended. Juarez had met with the leaders and formed a truce. There was no mention of Mendez.

Sid could picture him living in luxury somewhere, as he knew he had great wealth after confiscating the treasury of Diaz.

About ten that morning Rico got up. He was grateful for the coffee and rolls. Sid said, "Do you really sleep with all four of those girls?"

"Yes, they know I cannot get them pregnant, and they enjoy me as much as I enjoy them. I never have more than one at a time though. That would be immoral." Sid just shook his head and smiled.

I need to leave, Rico, I want to get back to Guadalajara and resume my medical practice."

"I'll see you off, Sid. We won't wake the girls." They left in Rico's buggy and he dropped him at the train station. His parting words were, "Please come see us every few months. The girls were quite fascinated with you."

"I'll come back, but just as show business is your life, my life is medicine. I am the happiest keeping people healthy and healing them."

"I understand, but promise me that you will return every three or four months. The girls will be looking for you."

133

CHAPTER 14

A NEW HOME

The train trip to Guadalajara was comfortable. Sid always liked riding on trains. The seats were comfortable, and the dining was excellent. It sure beat riding a horse for two days and camping out. He sat in his seat half asleep, wondering if there would ever be a steam machine that you could drive like a buggy.

It was morning now and they were stopping in a small town called Tonala, just a few miles from Guadalajara. Sid asked the conductor if he had time to stretch his legs. The conductor said, "We'll be here about ten minutes, so I think so."

Sid stepped off the train and walked along the depot platform. He saw a general store across the street and decided to look at their merchandise. He opened the door and a bell sounded above his head. It was common in small stores for the owner to live in the back and when someone entered the store, he would then come out to serve the person.

Sid's eye caught sight of a handgun that would fit under one's coat in a scabbard that fit neatly under one's armpit. He was admiring it when a woman's voice said, "That gun is for a gentleman like you. I bought it from a man who was broke. I gave him a good price and thought I could make a profit on it."

Sid looked around at a beautiful woman. Their eyes met and each gazed into each others eyes, and could not take their eyes away.

In an awkward moment, Sid said, "You seemed to have mesmerized me with your beauty, Senora."

"She smiled and said, "I felt the same way. Did you get off the train?"

"Yes. Just a chance meeting, a moment in time, where two people meet and feel something deep inside."

"Yes, I felt it, too, however, I'm married, and those feeling will have to stay just where they are. However, isn't it nice to have such a feeling if only for a moment?"

"I will always cherish this moment, and think of you when I'm traveling. Without asking the price Sid said, "I'll take the gun and scabbard."

Sid paid the lady and their hands touched as he handed her the money. When she gave him his change she touched his hands. He took off his coat, and put on the scabbard. She helped him and when she did, they came together spontaneously and held one another for a moment, then she pulled away and handed him his coat.

She said, "I'm glad you are on the train, Senor. I now have something to tell Father Abrea at my next confession."

"I wish I had time to make your confession very interesting."

"She smiled and said, "I will always remember you, Senor."

Sid asked, "Could I have your name? I want to have a name to go with my dreams of you."

"Yes, it's Julia, and what is your name?"

"Sid."

She said, "I have read of El Cid, he is a Spanish hero."

"Yes, but I spell my name with a "S.""

"You will still be my 'El Cid,' the hero of my dreams."

Later when he was on the train he thought, *"I didn't even ask her last name. I have seen more beautiful women, but she had something that pulled my heart strings. I will always dream of Julia. Not knowing her too well may be better for me."*

It was midmorning when they reached Guadalajara and Sid was still a bit cramped from a night on a train seat. As he was a bit cramped, he decided to walk to Dr. Contreras' office. The walk was about a mile and he limbered up before reaching the office.

Dr. Contreras was more than glad to see him. He said, "I was just thinking how you could help me. I am inundated with patients. Can you go to work immediately?"

Sid smiled and said, "It will be a pleasure Doctor. Let me wash up and put on a white coat."

Sid fit in nicely. He had patients all day long that were mostly women. This bothered Sid as he could see some of the women were infatuated with him. Dr. Contreras even kidded him about it."

After Sid had been there about two weeks, he received a message from a land dealer. The note said that he would like to meet him at his office the next day at ten in the morning. Sid was very busy, but he blocked out two hours and went to meet with the man.

When he arrived Maria, the woman who had saved him when he was at General Diaz's mansion, was sitting in a chair across from the land dealer. Sid was mildly surprised and said, "Buenos dais, Maria."

She said, "You remembered my name, Doctor Porter. How nice of you."

"I always remember beautiful women who I am close to, and we were close as I remember."

The land man, Senor Campos, introduced himself and said, "Maria will tell you the story of why you are here."

Maria said, "I am a first cousin of Carlos Mendez. He has purchased the mansion that General Diaz had for sell. General Diaz doesn't know it is Carlos who put up the money. The title has your name on it, Sidney Porter. Carlos says you and he own it together. He can never have his name on any document or they would confiscate it. So, he said that you were his good friend, and that you would own it with him.

"Maximilian built this place the first year he was emperor of Mexico. He brought an architect from France to design it. It is a unique palace with many hidden treasures. Carlos wants you to live there and enjoy all of its pleasures, which I might add are many. He has a bedroom there, although not quite as elaborate as yours. He stays here less than ten times a year, but when he is here, he likes to live big. He is very wealthy. He took most of his money from Diaz, but he also took much from the thieves that were with Maximilian."

Campos said, "Here are the papers you must sign. I will file your deed with the proper authorities and give you a copy of the deed."

As Sid was signing the papers he said, "Just give the deed to Maria, she will know where to store it. She is as much owner as I am. She runs the place."

Maria smiled and said, "If you are trying to woo me, it's working."

After the papers were signed, Sid left with Maria to the mansion. As they were walking, Maria said, "Let me tell you about the mansion. I was hired by Maximilian to be head housekeeper. He wanted me to also oversee the construction of it. He gave instructions to the builder that I could change and add anything. This gave me great power. I put in secret passageways all over the house, so the servants would not be meeting the owners in the hallways. I can't wait to show you your bedroom."

They arrived and were greeted by several of the servants and cooks. Maria introduced him as the new owner of the mansion. Many of the servants knew him, and he recognized several as he had met them at his medical office. The great room was enormous. Its ceiling was some forty feet high. It had numerous statues and the walls were covered with beautiful paintings and tapestries.

Maria said, "We will have time later for me to tell you about each room and its treasures. I know you must return to your work, but first I want you to see your bedroom."

It was on the second floor. Two marble staircases met midway up and then diverged in separate directions. It then went on up to the third floor which had several bedrooms.

At the end of one of stairs on the second floor was a large wooden door. It had been beautifully carved and lacquered. Maria opened the door to a spacious room. It had fifteen foot ceilings with three crystal chandeliers. The ceiling was painted with life-sized people and angels. It was breath taking. The walls were adorned with paintings and tapestries. There was a small booth that Sid opened the door. It had a place to kneel with candles burning on an alter. On the alter was a life size statue of the Virgin. Each side of the prayer booth were stained glass windows, as the small room protruded to the outside of the house.

There was a fireplace with a plush rug and couch in front of it. There was a large desk that faced the room. It had many books on the shelves in back of it. Sid picked up one of the books and noted they were all in French. The desk had extravagant quills and paper.

There were two stuffed chair with a side table between them for reading. It was placed by an outside window that provided a reader light. It also had lamps to illuminated it for reading at night.

The bed was immense. It had a canopy over it that was held up with four beautifully carved posts. Sid noticed the sheets were silk as were the pillowcases. It was a room fit for a king.

There was a bathroom off one side. It had a chandelier, also. The bathtub was made of brass. There were two washbasins that lay in a tiled counter top, with mirrors that covered the entire sink area. The commode was in a separate room off the bath with a door.

Sid noticed that on both sides of the bed, the reading chair and the desk had velvet ropes. He looked at Maria and she said, "Pull on one of the ropes."

Sid did, and a few moments later, one of the wall panels opened and a servant appeared.

Maria said, "This is Eduardo. He will be your valet. He and his brother spell each other in this duty. Other servants appear when you need something to drink or eat. Pull that lever next to the door panel."

Sid pulled it, and an elaborate bar came out with nearly every liquor he had ever seen."

"I know you have to get back Doctor Porter, but I wanted you to have something to think about while you're gone. We will be expecting your for dinner tonight. We serve dinner at seven o'clock.

"If you are wondering why you haven't seen my daughter, I sent her away yesterday to Mexico City to a school. I could tell the way she looked at you that I had better do something, or she would soon be in your bed."

Sid smiled and said, "You are very wise, Maria."

When he returned, he talked to Dr. Contreras and said, "I will be moving, Doctor. I have found a nice place where I want to live."

That night Maria told him that on Saturday nights, they entertained. People who were of the high society of Guadalajara were invited. Extra women were also there. Some were widows and some were young. All of these were beautiful. Maria did this to keep the affluent males happy.

There was a band of musicians who were very good. Liquor flowed and all danced. Many of the women wanted Sid to dance with them, so he danced most dances. He wished Rico were here with his four women. They could really entertain. After he was in his room he wrote Rico to bring his women and come for a visit. He said, "The place I have is large enough to house you all."

Dr. Contreras was at the party, but didn't realize that Sid owned the place. He just though Sid was a guest like himself.

Sid needed new clothes, and Maria told him where to go to buy them. This dealer sold only the best clothes. The prices were high, but Maria insisted that he go there. As a matter of fact, she went with him. Sid smiled to himself as he knew Maria liked to mother him.

She picked out three suits, and some clothes that were worn by the affluent men of Mexico. Sid didn't say a thing. He just let her pick out what she liked. She bought scarves, gloves, top coats, hats and underwear. The bill nearly buckled Sid's knees, but as he was about to pay, the owner of the shop said, "All of your clothes have been paid for."

"By whom," Sid asked.

"I am not a liberty to say."

Sid said, "Mendez."

Maria just smiled and said, "Your house has many services, Doctor."

Many of the items had to be tailored, but the dealer was an expert.

Sid had a nice body for a man. He was about five ten and was slim. The clothes fit him like a glove. Which made him attractive. Maria said, "Now, I will have to be by you a lot to keep the women away."

"I like some of them." Sid answered.

She then looked seriously at Sid and said, "I know a man

has needs. I have a couple of women who could meet those needs if you want."

Sid smiled and said, "No, Maria, I don't want those kind. When I make love to a woman I want to love her deeply. I was married once. I loved her deeply, but she died. I loved her from the time I was twelve years old, and never thought of another woman."

"It must have hurt to lose a woman that young."

"She wasn't that young. She was thirty years older than me. However, the age difference didn't affect our love."

"My, I have never heard of an age difference that acute except with men. They often prefer a woman twenty years younger, when they lose their first wife."

"There you are. What is the difference?"

Sid was going back the next day to pick up his clothes that had to be tailored. He was about to enter the store when he saw Julia, the woman from Tonale. She was walking toward him, and he just waited until she was nearly to him and said, "Hello, Julia."

She gasped at seeing Sid. She said, "I never thought we would see each other again. I am here to order some merchandise for our store."

"Do you have time for a coffee?"

She smiled and said, "I'll make time."

They sat across from one another and didn't speak. They just looked at one another. She broke the silence and said, "I have thought of you everyday since we last met."

"I can do better than that, I think of you about every hour. You did something to me."

"I know. My husband is twenty-four years older than me

and just uses me. There is never any love to it. I would leave him, but it is against God's will, and I cannot do that."

Sid said, "I guess I will have to wait until he dies."

"You must need a woman, Sid. Men seem to have to have a woman. Many need more than one. How can you go without one."

"If the one is you, Julia, I can go without by just thinking of you."

She said, "We need to keep up with one another, but not be too close to each other. I will have to confess this to father Abrea at my next confession."

"Don't do that, Julia. We have not sinned, and no one needs to know. God knows, and that is enough. He must have brought us together, or we would not have ever met."

"Do you really think so, Sid?"

"I know so, Julia."

"We must never say words or touch. If we can do that, it is not sin."

"I suppose you're right. I would love to say words and touch. I would like to give you my love and receive yours."

"Don't go further, Julia. It's hard for me like it is, don't make it worse."

"She smiled and said, "It is a fine thing to love. It is much better for me now. I have something to look forward to." A frown then came on her face. She said, "You may not want me by the time Louis dies."

"Let me tell you about my first wife. I saw her the first time when I was twelve years old. I fell in love with her instantly. I knew she would be the only woman I would ever love. She was married and had two daughters seven or eight years older than me."

"How much older was she than you, Sid?"

"Thirty years. But it made no difference. Her husband was sickly and died when I was sixteen. From the time I was twelve, we sat together in church. She thought of me as a son she never had, but I thought of her as the love of my life.

"When I was eighteen she hired me to be a hand at her ranch. Her daughters had married and left. She kept me around the house, mostly to do chores as she liked me to be around her.

"A drought came, and she had to lay off half of the other hands. I was the last hired so I had to be the first to be laid off. I went to the house the night before I left. I told her I loved her and had been in love with her since I was twelve. I told her I would write her a letter once a week. It would not be an ordinary letter, it would be a love letter.

"That must have pulled her heart strings. We kissed goodbye. Not a short kiss, but a passionate love kiss. I kissed her twice and then left. I came to Mexico. After a year or so, she wrote and told me to come home as she wanted to marry me. We lived nearly two years together in bliss. I could not love her enough.

"However, one of her daughters came home as her husband was caught with a neighbor's wife and was shot dead. I went with the daughter to settled her affairs. On the way back, we were attacked by three men. They would have killed us, but I got away. While I was planning my attack on them, they raped her. I managed to kill one of them and wound the another who died later. I let the third go as he had not taken Alta's daughter.

We never told anyone about the rape as it was so embarrassing for her. However, she became pregnant. Neither of us said anything to my wife about the rape, and when her daughter began to show, she thought we had slept together. We didn't realize that she thought that. She asked me to leave. I thought she had just grown tired of me, so I left. After I was gone, her daughter told her about the rape. She then realized what had happened, but it was too late.

"We lost contact with one another for about a year or more, then I received a letter from her daughter that she was dying of cancer. I returned the day after she died. I loved her very deeply and have not loved anyone since.

"I did sleep with one woman because she needed me badly. She was so scared she trembled. I knew I must make love to her to calm her. I did it for her, not me. I did receive pleasure from it, but there was no love to it. That was the only time I strayed.

"So, you know my life story. I have never loved anyone until I met you. So, you see, if I can wait eight years for a wife I thought I may never have. Waiting for you will be easy. I'll just kiss my pillow each night and think of you."

Julia said, "That was the most wonderful story I have ever heard. I wish that she hadn't have died and that you were still making love to her every night. That's how much I love you. I want you to be happy."

"That is something, Julia. I feel the same. It doesn't bother me that you have to bed your husband. A wife must do that and I understand. When he makes love to you, pretend it is me. You may receive some pleasure from it."

She smiled and said, "That would be adultery, so I cannot do that. I will think of you though, but not when I am in bed."

They parted and Sid asked himself, *"Why is it, that every woman I love, I have to wait years for. She'll probably die before Louis."*

CHAPTER 15

A TRAITOR CAUSES TROUBLE

General Diaz had spies around Mexico to keep him informed about what was going on. One of the spies was in Guadalajara. It was a woman who Diaz had bedded many times. She loved him, but he did not love her. He kept her dangling so he could get information.

The woman was Leslie Gomez. She worked at a place near the mansion. She knew Maria was a cousin to Carlos Mendez and that Dr. Porter was Carlos' friend. She had a friend who she slept with that worked in the government land office.

When the transaction transferring the title of the mansion came through his office, he saw that Sidney Porter now owned it. He told Leslie, and she remembered that Doctor Porter was a friend of Mendez. She wrote a letter to Diaz, and he sent her fifty pesos.

Diaz thought if he could get Juarez to believe that Porter was a traitor, he might imprison Porter, and then he might get his property back. Diaz wrote a long letter to Juarez that told him about Mendez's and Porter's relationship. He said that Porter should be punished as a revolutionary.

Juarez did not trust Diaz as he had falsely accused people he didn't like before. One of them was shot and later Juarez learned of his innocence. This troubled Juarez and he swore he would thoroughly check out everyone who was accused of being a traitor, especially when Diaz was the accuser."

Sid received an official letter from President Juarez to come to the palace and appear before him. Sid had no choice. He packed his finest clothes and went to Mexico City.

He appeared and Juarez said, "You have been accused of treason. I have a letter that states you are a friend of Carlos Mendez. What do you have to say about that?"

Sid said, "I am a friend of Mendez. We met during a siege between Mendez and Diaz. Diaz was run off. There were several wounded men from both sides. I am a doctor and I helped all I could. I am not political, I am a doctor sworn to heal people which I did.

"Later, Diaz tried to have me hung for it, but Mendez saved me from being hung and defeated Diaz and his men. In order to not be hung, Diaz told Mendez about a stash of treasure that he had hidden. It was great wealth, with many arms that Diaz had hidden from you and your party. Stolen goods as you would.

"Mendez let him go and he came straight to you with

a fabricated story. I am not on any side. I am an American citizen working here in Mexico as a doctor to heal people.

"I live in a mansion that Mendez paid for, but cannot own because he is branded a traitor. However, the people do not think of him as a traitor. They love him, because he takes care of the poor, the sick and the aged. He is a good man, that I call a friend."

Juarez said, "I see you are not against me or my party. I will inform Diaz that you are a friend of the state and he will not bother you."

"You say these words, but can you trust Diaz?" He sent you a letter hoping you would hang me. I know you are a good ruler and the people love you. However, Diaz is a scoundrel and I, and the people, do not trust him."

Sid was let go and he went straight to Rico's house. Rico was glad to see him. He said, "After our performance tonight we will have dinner and a party at my house.

The show was good and the dinner exquisite. At the dinner, Sid told them why he was in Mexico City and how President Juarez had exonerated him from Diaz's accusation. They traveled to Rico's house. After Rico had poured them a drink, Salendra asked, "When are you going to give me a baby, Sid?"

Sid laughed and said, "It wouldn't be fair unless I gave you all a baby."

They were all laughing, when soldiers broke into the house. They had rifles pointed at Sid. Their leader said, "You will come with us."

Sid said just one word to Rico, "Diaz."

Sid could do nothing. He just took his coat and left.

Outside a coach was waiting for him. Two more soldiers were inside the coach with drawn pistols. They were then off. Sid had no idea where they were going. They traveled all night, just stopping to rest the horses at intervals. Sid could tell they were heading north when he was let out to relieve himself when they rested the horses.

He asked one of the guards where they were headed. The guard whispered, "Monterrey."

At dawn they came to a way station. He was brought in and was fed with the soldiers. The way station manager said nothing as he knew full well the savagery of soldiers under General Diaz.

It took five days to reach Monterrey where General Diaz had his headquarters. Sid was put into a prison there. Many other prisoners were there. Sid came in the middle of the night. The next morning five of the prisoners were led out, lined up against a wall and were shot. Many watched from the jail window, but Sid did not. He knew what was happening. They were fed only bread and water.

One of the prisoners said, "We have nothing to lose as we will all be shot sooner or later. We must act together. When they are feeding us tonight, we will try to take the guards. Some of us will probably be shot, but it's the only way." The rest agreed and some planning was done. Sid kept to himself and said nothing.

That night when the soldiers came to give them their food, one of the prisoners grabbed the one guard and another grabbed another. Two other guards had their pistols out and killed two of the prisoners before they were both overwhelmed and killed. The prisoners now had weapons. They went out from the inner cell area to the outer cell area. There they were met with more force. They killed two more prisoners before the prisoners overwhelmed the other guards and took their weapons.

The prisoners were fifteen or better and they all now had arms, because they had broken into a cabinet that had many rifles and much ammunition.

Sid retrieved a pistol and a scabbard with about sixty to seventy rounds of ammunition from one of the guards lying on the floor He also took the guard's wallet. He knew that staying with the prisoners would be a gamble, so as soon as they were outside, most of them went for horses that were in a stable near the jail.

Sid did not. He went up a side street and went to the poorest part of Monterrey. The Alvarado family lived south of town as did the Romero family, but Sid knew the roads would be watched soon. He also knew they would search both hacienda thoroughly. When he had been in Monterrey with Sanchez, he pointed out the poor part of town. Sid knew he must find refuge. He also knew that poor people are kinder to those that are downtrodden. He was thinking he had to lie low for a week or so. When he rested he examined the guard's wallet as he knew he must have money. The guard had several pesos, but not what Sid had hoped for.

He traveled for a mile or two, and as he neared the edge of the city, he decided to hide in a barn until people started getting up. At dawn, a woman started for the barn and Sid showed her five pesos. She smiled at him and said, "Are you hiding from the soldiers?"

"Yes. I have just escaped from the prison. I was to be shot today. I am innocent, but General Diaz hates me."

"That pig had one of my cousins killed. I hate him. I will hide you in my house a few days until they quit looking for you."

"I have money to pay for my keep. I know they will search all the houses. Do you have some place to hide me?"

She said, "Si, my husband made a place for emergencies. It is under the floor in my bedroom. He took out the boards and made a hiding place. No one can find it as its cover matches the other boards perfectly. It is just large enough for one to lie in the bed he made."

"Will your husband agree to hid me?"

"Yes, because he is dead and has no say. He would have never agreed to hide a stranger, but you have a nice look about you. Are you hungry?"

"Yes, they only fed us bread and very little of that."

"Come into the house before someone sees you."

In the house, she made Sid a good breakfast. He was very hungry and everything tasted scrumptious. While he was eating, she went out to the barn to do her chores. When she returned, she showed him the place he would be kept if the soldiers came.

She said, "I am Juanita."

"I am Sid," he answered. "I will always treasure our friendship, because you saved my life."

The soldiers didn't come that day. At night Juanita said, "The soldiers will not come tonight. I will make you a pallet next to my bed, so that if the soldiers were to come we can quickly put you in the place under my bed. There is water and jerky there that will last you a day or so."

Sid asked, "Do you have neighbors who will come to see you?"

"Yes, but I will put you in the closet in my room, and you will be safe there. I will leave an olla of water and some tortillas for you.

No one came to visit Juanita, but near dusk they could see soldiers coming into the area to search.

Their captain said, "Search thoroughly. Even look up under the skirts of the women," and they all laughed. He added, "Find you a woman to sleep with, and report back here tomorrow morning."

The company had over twenty men who spread out. Juanita and Sid could see one of the soldiers riding toward Juanita's house. Juanita lit two candles, one in the front room and the other in her bedroom as the soldier tied his horse to the rail.

They had no time to put Sid in the hiding place, so he went to the closet to hide. He noticed that Juanita had two chairs in the closet, so she could step on them and reach the top shelf. Sid set one of the chairs out in front of the closet. He also noticed a rope that was coiled and hung on peg. A plan began to form in his mind.

Juanita had put on a blouse that was low cut and showed the tops of her ample bosom. As the soldier approached, she opened the door with a smile. She took him by the hand and led him into her bedroom. She said, "take down your pants and sit in that chair," as she pointed to the one in front of the closet.

The soldier followed her instructions. She then put on some perfume then knelt in front of the soldier and began giving him what he wanted. She had seen Sid with the rope and knew what he was going to do. She made noise by smacking her lips and groaning some so that it would cover any noise that Sid might make with the rope.

Sid stood on the remaining chair and by leaning out of the closet, he was able to put the rope over a beam that ran through the house. He then took the loop at the end and threw it over the soldier's head and drew the loop tight. He jumped from the chair holding the rope and it drew the soldier up. The soldier had to stand on the chair to keep breathing. Juanita came and kicked the chair out from under the soldier, while Sid held the rope tightly in a sitting position.

The soldier struggled, trying to loosen the rope with his hands, but it was no use. After just a minute or two he quit struggling and his hands went beside him. Sid still held the rope tightly for another minute or two, then let him down.

Juanita felt his pulse and said, "He's dead." As they looked at the dead soldier, Juanita said, "Let's wait until after midnight and take him to the church. It's only a block from here. We can then take the rope and put it over the oak tree limb and make it look like he committed suicide."

She pulled his pants up and took out his wallet. There were a few pesos which she took, then returned the wallet. After midnight, Sid put the soldier over his horse and followed Juanita to the church. Sid threw the rope over a high branch then placed the loop once more over the soldier's head and they drew him up high enough so that it would look like he put the rope over his head and then spurred his horse so that he would hang.

There was a rope hung on his saddle and Sid took that to make it look like he used his own rope.

Sid said, "I can never repay you for what you did for me."

Juanita said, "I think you can. I want a baby very badly. I know I am not comely enough to entice a good looking man like you to give me one. I want to have your baby. It will comfort me in my old age. I am nearing the point at my age that will end my chances for a baby.

"You will not be blamed by God, as it is a gift to me and not fornication. Will you do it for me.".

She looked at Sid with such pleading in her eyes that he said, "I will give you that baby, Juanita. I not only owe it to you, but I give it to you with an loving heart."

Sid nodded and she handed him a night shirt. They were now in bed. Sid said a prayer. "Father I do this for Juanita. Please bless her and give her the child she so dearly wants. If I am sinning, please forgive us both."

After they were lying on their backs, Juanita said, "I will tell the people that the soldier raped me, and that is why he committed suicide. They will think the child is from the soldier."

She made love to Sid throughout the night. He was exhausted by her as she had let out her desire that had been pent up since her husband had died. Just as Sid woke, she was on him again. Sid thought, *"This woman has more desire than any woman I have ever known."* She had desire, but her greatest desire was to make sure she got pregnant.

Sid stayed five more days. She literally wore him out. She

knew methods to bring him alive that he never knew existed. He thought, *"Now I know why her husband died, she loved him to death."*

The sixth day Sid prepared for his trip. Juanita had given him some of her husband's clothes. They were off-white pants and a pullover white shirt. He wore her husband's sombrero and put his clothes along with some tortillas and jerky in a nap sack. He left late, because Juanita wanted him to make love to her again before he left.

He walked cautiously looking for roadblocks, but the soldiers had been recalled as all but one of the prisoners had been captured, then shot. Diaz was furious when he found that Sid had escaped and could not be found.

* * *

When the soldiers had taken Sid from Rico's house, the girls and Rico talked about what to do. Rico said, "I will go to President Juarez tomorrow and report that Diaz's soldiers took Sid. He may not see me, but I will write a letter everyday telling him of the abduction.

The President was too busy to see Rico, but Rico left the letter. He came everyday that week and always the answer was the same. The aide to the president had never informed him of Rico coming to see him.

Rico had all the girls write the president informing of the abduction. He then had had everyone in the troupe write him. Rico knew that his aide wasn't telling the president, because he knew some action would have been taken.

When the many letters began to come, the aide knew he

could not keep from telling the president, because he himself may be fired for keeping the abduction quiet.

Rico still came every day and finally the aide told the president that a man had been coming to see him for two weeks straight, and that he was now getting ten to twenty letters each day about an abduction.

President Juarez said, "Why didn't you inform me, so I could decide whether to see this man or not?"

The aide was a spy for General Diaz and he knew this might come out. President knew Rico as he had seen him perform several times. He apologized for his aide and said, "I had no idea you had come to see me everyday for two weeks. You must have something very important to tell me."

Rico then told him about Sid's abduction by Diaz's soldiers. He also added that he thought that his aide was a confident of the general's or he would have let him in or at least shown him the letters.

Juarez said, "You say this happened over two weeks ago?"

"Yes, your Excellency. Diaz may have had him shot by now, as I hear he is shooting anyone he does not like, and he hates Doctor Porter."

"I will send a wire at once telling Diaz that I have knowledge of him taking Doctor Porter and will expect him to deliver Doctor Porter to me this week in person. He added that if Doctor Porter is injured in any manner, he will be held accountable."

Diaz was shocked when he received the wire. He had no idea that Doctor Porter was a friend of the president. He started thinking how he could cover this incident. He discussed it with an aide of his.

The aide said, "You can tell him that it was a mistake and as soon as you realized what his men had done, you set him free. Doctor Porter is still at large, and no one has seen him. What can the president do? It was all just a mistake."

"That would work if Doctor Porter never sees the president again, but if he does, I'm dead or at best exiled from Mexico. Intensify the search. Someone is hiding him."

"We have had all modes of transportation watched since his escape, General. He might have disguised himself, and got through the road blocks."

"I don't think so. I think he is still in or around Monterrey. Have all the haciendas searched again, especially the affluent people. I don't think he would mingle with the peons."

* * *

Sid had made it to a barn close to the Alvarado estate. He had decided to stay the rest of the night there. In the morning he would catch someone going to the Alvarado estate. Hopefully, it would be a wagon delivering merchandise to them.

It worked, and a wagon passed the barn. Sid covertly hopped into the back of the wagon and covered himself with a tarp. The wagon was stopped at the gate, then let in because the driver was well known as he had delivered things routinely to the Alvarado family for many years.

When the wagon came to a stop, Sid hopped out and made his way to a shed unseen. He then changed into his regular clothes. They were a bit wrinkled, but he smoothed them out the best he could. He put on his American hat and walked to the front door.

The butler answered the door and he recognized Sid from previous visits. He showed him to the parlor and left to inform the Senor and Senora of Sid's presents.

They greeted Sid with warmth. Sid then told his story. He said, "Diaz will not rest until I am captured. If you take me in, you will be risking your family, Senor."

Senor Alvarado said, "Maybe you would be safer at Senor Ramos' hacienda. Rafael is much more innovative with these things than I am."

Sid could tell that Senor Alvarado didn't want him to stay, so he said, "That is a good idea, Senor. I will rest up and leave tonight, if that is okay."

Alvarado wanted him to leave immediately, but could think of nothing. He showed Sid a room to sleep in, then said, "If the soldiers come, go out that window and hide in the cornfield until they leave.

Around five in the afternoon, Sid awoke. He dressed and came down stairs. Alvarado was waiting for him. He had him fed and then gave him a sack of food and a canteen. He had his buggy ready and took him to the main road. He had sent his workers to make sure there were no soldiers anywhere.

At the main road Alvarado stopped and said, "Via con dias, Doctor Porter."

Sid just nodded and left walking. Alvarado hadn't offered him a horse as he didn't want the horse traced back to him.

It was dark now and only a half moon to light his way. As he walked he tried to think of pleasant things. He thought of Juanita and her passion. He then thought that maybe she wanted a child so badly that she wanted to make sure she was pregnant. He smiled to himself and thought, "*If every woman was like her, men would be like women and stay aloof from them."*

It was eight to ten miles to Senor Ramos' hacienda. It took most of the night to get there as Sid had to be careful of where he walked. About five in the morning he knew he was getting close. He could see a campfire burning ahead of him. He hid in some trees and waited. By dawn he could tell it was a company of soldiers bivouacked.

Sid drew back another quarter of a mile to a stream that had steep banks. He found a way to the bottom and looked for a place to hide. He found just what he wanted. It was a cave with a very small entrance. He went back on his trail to make sure he didn't leave any footprints. He then brought rocks to the small entrance in order to close the entrance and make it look like just part of the creek bank. When he was in the cave and the entrance was closed he laid down and slept. He was awakened by men talking. He could tell it was soldiers searching the creek. He just laid there and fell asleep again.

It was nearly dark when he pushed the rooks away. He ate and drank from the stream. He then cautiously made his way toward the Ramos estate. He had decided to approach from the opposite direction. He widely circled the estate as not to disturb the dogs that he knew were there. He had kept some jerky to feed the dogs if they came to him.

It was dusk as he made his way to a barn. The dogs came, but quickly found a friend, as they ate the jerky. He petted one of them and they never barked again. He made his way to the house when it was dark. He looked into the windows to make sure no soldiers were there.

Sid knocked and a servant answered the door. She

recognized Sid and gave him a large smile and told him to come in. She went to get Rafael and Cloressa.

They were glad to see him. Rafael said, "The soldiers were here today. I now know why. Did they have you?"

"Yes, but I escaped over a week ago. A kind lady hid me for nearly a week. I owe her my life."

Rafael said, "I don't think the soldiers will be back. They know nothing of our friendship or that you were ever here. They searched like I have never seen anyone search. They went through every field and stand of trees for miles around the rancho. They questioned all our servants and vaqueros. They all said the same thing, that they had seen no strangers, and no one had been to the ranchero lately.

"They never said who they were looking for and we had no idea it was you. Why is General Diaz looking for you?"

Sid then spun his story. Clorressa asked, "Have you eaten?"

"No, I am very hungry."

Rafael and Clarress stayed with him while he ate. Sid asked, "Do you think the soldiers will return?"

"No, they searched thoroughly and were satisfied. We sit pretty far away, and they had road blocks, I am told, for over a week. We heard of the jail break, but someone said everyone was caught and shot." He laughed and added, "I see one person escaped though.

Sid said, I need to get to Mexico City to see the President. He understands the situation between Diaz and me. I think he will safeguard me from Diaz. However, I thought that before, but Diaz's hate for me is stronger than his fear. I will ask Mendez to handle him. That is the only way I will be safe."

Rafael said, "They will be looking for you to go to Mexico City. Diaz has hundreds of spies that would turn you in for the money they would get from Diaz. I suggest you travel to Matamoros on the coast, then catch a ship to Vera Cruz. From there you can travel to Mexico City."

"That sounds like good advice, however, I will have to borrow some money from you to make the trip."

"No problem, my friend. I will look around for someone going to Matamoros. There is much trade from the sea to Monterrey."

It was five days before Rafael found a merchant who had wagons returning to Matamoros. Sid was hired to drive one of the wagons. There were ten wagons in the group and all were friendly. The trip took five days.

CHAPTER 16

A SEA VOYAGE AND LOVE

At Matamoros, Sid found a ship that was heading for Vera Cruz. He asked if he could go as a seaman and work for his travel. The captain turned him down, as he had no experience. However, he was taken as a passenger. The ship was a freighter, but also had accommodations of five cabins. The ship had a lounge for the passengers that served drinks, and entertained the passengers. The passengers were all couples except one. That was a woman about Sid's age taking her mother to Vera Cruz. She was quite interesting as she wore expensive clothes and a beautiful diamond ring. She also sported a gold bracelet that had diamonds on it.

After the first nights dinner, Sid went to the lounge and ordered a brandy to compliment the exquisite meal. He had just sat down, when the two women came in. Others were there and the only places available was next to Sid. The older woman sat away leaving the younger only one place to sit and that was by Sid.

Sid smiled and said, "I'm Sid Porter, Ma'am."

She smiled a gorgeous smile and said, "I am Deloris Juarez and this is my mother Senora Gomez."

Sid stood and took the Senora's hand, then sat down again. There was an awkward silence then Deloris said, "What do you do, Senor Porter?"

"I'm a doctor. My office is in Guadalajara."

She turned and said, "My, mother, we are in good company."

"Are you traveling for pleasure or business, Senora Juarez?"

"Both I must say. Mother is going to see her sister and I wanted to come along as I haven't been in Mexico City for sometime. My late husband worked for the President."

"Was he related to the President?"

"Yes, he was a nephew. However, he also was a doctor of law and aided the president in legal matters."

"What a coincidence, I'm traveling to see the president on a private matter. However, I will also be traveling again to my practice in Guadalajara. May I offer you ladies a drink?"

"Thank you, we both like rum and cola, but light on the rum."

Sid left and shortly returned with their drinks. As he sat, Deloris asked, "Is there a Mrs. Porter, doctor?"

"There was, but she died some months ago."

"Oh, how sad. Had you been married long?"

"Yes, but we had been separated the past two years. I reached her the day after she died, so I was unable to say goodbye."

"My husband was killed by a treacherous villain, General Diaz. He told the president it was a mistake, but it wasn't. He did it because I slapped his face when he made a lascivious pass at me. He could not kill me, so he killed my husband."

General Diaz captured me in Mexico City, and brought me to Monterrey where he was hoping to have me shot, but I managed to escape."

"Yes, I recall the prison break. They said everyone was recaptured and shot, but I see the report was in error. You must be very resourceful, Doctor Porter."

"Please call me, Sid, as we now know our life stories."

Senora Gomez said, "I would like to lie down as I am tired."

They rose as did Sid. Senora Gomez was nearly at the hatch when Deloris whispered, "I'll meet you at the bow in a few minutes."

Sid was flattered, and whispered, "I'll be waiting."

They left and Sid had another drink thinking it would be sometime before Deloris put her mother to bed, refreshed herself then make some excuse to leave.

Sid smiled to himself and thought, "*She was very open to me. More open that I have known strange women to be. I wonder if she has a motive, after all, I'm not that attractive.*"

Sid was wrong. Deloris was captivated by his good looks. His suit fit him marvelously and she was more than interested.

After he finished his drink he made his way to the bow and Deloris was waiting. He thought, "*Wow! She is interested.*"

Deloris smiled and said, "I thought you had jilted me already."

Sid said, "No man would jilt such a lovely lady."

She then said, "I hate to be so forward, it is really not like me. However, I find that you interest me greatly. I am drawn to you. I have heard how romantic shipboard romances can be, and now I find myself wanting to experience that."

"I have never been on a ship and never heard of shipboard romances, but I think I can learn easily, what should I do?"

"Let's look at the moon and stars, then get close to one another."

At that time they could hear another couple coming so they parted. Sid thought, *"I can't become involved with this woman. She would want more than I want to give. I still think of Julia. She will be my wife, ultimately. We love each other.*

They walked back to the lounge and had a drink. The bartender had made a fruit cocktail that was delicious. He said, "Let me warn you. These drinks will slip up on you and you'll hate yourself in the morning," everyone laughed, but heeded his advice.

They didn't see each other the next night, as her mother was ill. Before disembarking Sid said, "Maybe we will see each other again, Goodbye." He had done this so that no addresses could be exchanged.

Sid went directly to Rico's house. Rico was extremely glad to see him. They told each other what had happened.

Sid said, "You are a true friend, Rico. I will always treasure our friendship.

That night Sid went to Rico's and the girl's performance. They were terrific. They had added some new numbers and changed the show a lot. After the show they dined at the same restaurant and then went to Rico's house.

During diner Sid retold his story. He looked a Rico and said, "A truer friend a man could not have."

Rico said while they were walking, "Sid, you know the girls have a strong liking for you."

"That may be true, but I have a love now that I must be true to."

"Tell me about it."

"I always seem to love someone who I cannot marry. My love is married to a man twenty years her senior and has no love for him. However, she does have love for our Lord and Savior, so we never see each other alone. It is always in public. I will just be patient and maybe the Lord will give her to me."

"That is a shame, Sid. You are a deep fellow. I could feel that almost immediately when we met. I don't think I have ever had a friend that I liked better. I know the girls like you."

Sid said, "I am going to see President Juarez tomorrow. Will you come with me?"

"It would be an honor, Sid."

The next day they went to the palace and were received and let in to see the President. The meeting with President Juarez was fruitful. He sent a telegram to Diaz after the meeting to come to Mexico City and report to him. The president's aide also wrote a telegram. He told Diaz he may be shot, so disappear."

Diaz never answered the telegrams, and did just what the aide suggested and went to Vera Cruz where he had some of his wealth, and some friends who leeched off him.

Sid was now on the train home. He was able to visit Julia when the train stopped at Tonala. He had only ten minutes. Her husband was in the back drinking, so they were alone.

They just looked at one another saying nothing. Just getting to be together was enough. As Sid was leaving she whispered, you are so beautiful."

When he was on the train again, he thought, *I feel no remorse for sleeping with Juanita. I wonder if she will have my baby. I will have to check on that sometime."*

Dr. Contreras said, "I am so glad you returned. You seem to appear when I need you the most. The women have been complaining about you being gone. Half are in love with you and the other half adore you."

Sid said, "They must all have dreadful lives."

Contreras looked up and said, "I think you have hit upon something. If we could cure their mental states, their physical state might improve. Let's start delving into their private lives and see if we can help them."

"I'm afraid to do that, Doctor."

"What is life if you don't take a chance once in awhile. We can always back off if we find it is something we shouldn't do."

"Only because I respect you so much, will I do this."

The next day a Senora Mantos came to see Sid. She did not appear to be ailing, but she complained about her shoulder. As Sid was rubbing her bare shoulder he asked, "Are you and your husband close?"

She was shocked and said, "Why do you ask such a question?"

"It has to do with your health, Senora. If you have a healthy home life your health is much better."

She then broke down and said, "We sleep in different rooms. I know he sees other women."

"Let me give you some advice. Make sure you tend to him

gently like you did when you were first married. When he is ready to go to bed, come to him and say you are lonely and need a hug. See how that goes. If he hugs you, then move in closer and tell him you want to kiss him. If that works go to his room and sleep with him. I think life will be much better for you both, if you can recapture some of the love you once had for one another."

The Senora was looking out the window and said, "I did love him. He was everything to me. I will try what you say, doctor. I think you are onto something."

At the end of the first day, the doctors met and discussed what went on. Dr. Contreras said, "I suggested to a woman much younger than me, to be more sensual with the one she loves. She turned and put her arms around me and attempted to kiss me."

Sid was drinking a drink and spit it all over himself laughing. When he gathered himself he said, "What happened then?"

"I told her that I meant her husband. She said she was in love with me, and just wanted to show it, when I asked her to be more sensual. I said, 'Your love is miss directed. You think you love me, because I help you, but it is gratitude, not love you feel. You have confused the two. If you will direct your love to your husband he will probably return your love. I told her this happens with many of my patients. It is not me they really love, it is the fact that I have helped them, and they confuse love with gratitude.

"She then though a minute and looked at me and blurted out, "My husband does not make love to me anymore.""

"I told her to feed him some liquor, and then put on a sexy

169

nightgown and some sweet perfume. Lean over him and kiss him around the ears, the take him to bed.

"She said she would try it. So I think I am making some progress."

They discussed every patient, and asked each other for advice. Sid suggested they keep a log on every patient. He said, "I know this is time consuming, but I see it as being helpful if we categorize each event so we can refer back to them."

They did this and began building a file. They read each others files when they met a case that was similar.

Three months passed and he received a letter from Rico. He said, "I'm going to be a father and you an uncle. I thought I was sterile, but I have been taking a drug that a doctor put me onto, and low and behold Salendra is pregnant. Now all the girls want a baby. I couldn't be more pleased."

Three months later he got a letter from Rico and it said that Tico and Landra were pregnant. They were all delighted. Sid thought, *"That house is going to have babies crying night and day. I will conveniently be busy if asked to come."*

Sid and Dr. Contraras were extremely busy. When they were having a cocktail after work, they discussed what to do about it.

Sid said, "Let's advertise at the medical school in Mexico City that there is two openings for young doctors. If we get a response or two, I'll go and interview them, then try to convince them what a wonder clinic we have and what a wonderful place Guadalajara is to live."

Sid again went to Mexico City. He had written Rico that he was coming. He was again greeted by the five and now six.

Tico was showing and rubbed her stomach and said, "He's wanting to get out. He kicks so hard that I want him out."

When they were at Rico's place, Queta said she was pregnant. So, everyone of Rico's women were or were going to be mothers. Rico was elated. They spent their time thinking of names. To get away, Sid told that he had come to interview doctors as their clinic was overwhelmed. He excused himself and went to the medical school.

Both the doctors he met were young, but knew their stuff. He hired both and set a time to be in Guadalajara.

Sid was glad that he didn't have to return to Rico's house as he said he was going home.

CHAPTER 17

LIVING THE GOOD LIFE

One Friday, Sid decided to pay Teresa Lopez a visit at lake Chapala. He rented a buggy and left Saturday morning very early. He arrived at dusk and drove straight to the Clinic. He was met at the door by a four year old boy who grinned and said, "Buenos Notches," to Sid. He looked up and there was Teresa smiling at him. She said, "Say hello to your son, Sid."

Sid was shocked. He said, "Is he really my son?"

She said, "He is Sidney Porter, Jr."

Sid was stunned. She said, "I knew I was pregnant before you left, but you were so distraught that I thought it would be better if I waited. I knew you would return. You love me too much not to. I know you are not in love with me and never could be, but I knew you would come. By the way, how's your sweetheart?"

"I went back and we were married. We had a blissful two years, then tragedy struck. She had a daughter who lost her husband and came home to live. Alta and I decided that it would be best if I went with her daughter to settle her affairs and then she would live with us on the ranch.

"On our trip back, we were attacked by three men. I got away, but the daughter was raped by the men before I could get in position to help her. I shot the men and we returned to the ranch. It was such an embarrassing thing for her that we never mentioned the rape to my wife or anyone.

"Four months later the daughter turned up pregnant. My wife thought we had slept together and told me to leave the ranch. Two days after that, her daughter realized she had kicked me out and told her about the rape. She was very sorry, but I was gone. They tried to find me, but didn't have any idea where I was.

"By chance I checked the mail in Guadalajara a few years later. There was a letter for me, telling that my wife was dying of cancer. I returned one day after she died. She left a letter telling me how much she loved me."

"That is a sad story. Did you marry again?"

"No, but I have another story. I was captured by General Diaz and he took me back to Monterrey to be shot. I escaped and a woman took me in and saved my life by hiding me at great peril to her own life. She wanted a baby, so I agreed to give her one. So now there are two Sid Porter, Juniors."

"You're probably the nicest man in the world. I know you didn't do it for the sex. You only bedded me because I was so scared and that was the only way you could calm me."

"Oh, I enjoyed the sex. I guess everyone does."

"Will you ever have a wife?"

"Yes, I met someone and we fell in love. It was an instantaneous thing. We have seen each other for two years now, but have never been intimate, because she is married. He is twenty years older that she is. We have to wait until he dies."

Teresa said, "With your luck, she may die first."

"I've thought of that. Only God knows. Maybe it is because of my transgressions that I am being punished."

"No, I feel you have not sinned. You are just a nice man." She laughed and said, "I wonder who the next Sid, junior will be."

Sid said, "I hope the next Sid will be from the woman I love, but she may be too old to conceive by then."

"I hope you will sleep with me again. One child just makes for a lonely child."

Sid said, "I guess that is the boon of my life. I will probably leave ten children on this earth and none will call me father."

They went to eat and Sid slept with her that night. The next morning Teresa said, "I have made a lot of money, Sid. Not just a lot, a whole lot. Do you need some?"

"No, my practice in Guadalajara is very lucrative."

"Well, I thought I'd ask. By the way, everyone calls me Senora Porter. I hope you don't mind. I just tell people we are separated for long spans of time as you have a practice in Guadalajara."

"If you are ever in Guadalajara, you are welcomed to stay with me. Do you remember that palace that Maximilian built?"

"That huge mansion?"

"Yes. Carlos Mendez bought it for me. He pays for all

the upkeep and servants. I have nothing to do but live in the greatest palace in Mexico, and be waited on like a king. It has so many bedrooms I have never counted them. So when you come, bring your best clothes as we have a fiesta every Saturday night. Mendez comes around about five to ten times a year. I really like him." "He must like you pretty well, also. Sid, I will never put any demands on you. Thank you for giving me another child. I'm hoping for a girl this time. I hope you will father ten children for me."

Sid smiled. He left that day and drover back. He pondered *"I wonder what Alta would say about all this. It would have never happened, but for the rape of Lisa."*

He then thought, *"When Doctor Contreras decides to retire, I will invite Teresa to come and take his place.*

* * *

Diaz had a secret place in Guadalajara. He had it for years under his mother's maiden name. It was occupied by his sister, Maria, and her daughter, Chanel. Maria liked Diaz because he gave her the house and money to live on.

The daughter hated him, because he took her when she was but ten years old. He continued this until he left when she was twelve. Chanel told her mother, but her mother said she needed to be nice to Jamie. It ruined Chenel's love for men and she hated most men, especially Jamie Diaz. It was not just his raping her, it was his cruelty to others. He enjoyed giving people pain, both physically and mentally.

They hadn't seen Diaz since he left for Monterrey, but now

he had returned. He had disguised himself as he was afraid word may get back to Juarez.

When he arrived, Maria put her arms around him and hugged him, but Chanel stayed away from him with hate in her eyes. Diaz could see this, and decided to wait until he got her alone.

Chanel had grown to be a shapely woman, and this was not lost on Diaz's lascivious leers at her. However, he knew a woman could be dangerous. He once had been stabbed by a woman he raped. He loved women who resisted him. He would beat them until they submitted to him. He would continue beating them until they became so afraid of him that they would do anything for him. He usually cast them off after that.

Chanel had thought of Diaz for some years on how she would deal with him. She wanted to get him in a vulnerable position and then capture him. She would starve him until he would do anything for her, just like she had seen him do other women.

She took her education seriously, and with the time others spent on male companionship, she had extra time to study. This put her at the top of her class, and the teachers thought she was gifted. However, most of her acumen came from long hours of study.

Chanel was permitted to attend college, where she again excelled. She was noticed by a financier named, Guido Estrada, who had accumulated great wealth. He had learned the secret of using smart men to make him money. He saw in Chanel a budding talent that he could mold into his cartel. He had covered himself from people in government by placing a number of men's names on the title of his business. All of these names were factious as he was the only owner. When he met with government leaders, he told them that he was just the spokesman for a number of men who wished to stay anonymous. The government accepted that, and when they made demands, he would say that he could not make a decision without the owners okay.

This would give him time to maneuver. He would then have one of his men corner one of the members or the government who was making the demand, and either pay they off, or intimidate them in someway. He now had most of those in government in his pocket. Estrada was a small man, but was brilliant. He even had intuitive powers in business dealing.

He married early as his father had left him a legacy. His wife was a mild woman who stayed in the background. However, she had the ability to make Estrada love her completely. She was very talented in that area, so Estrada never strayed. He had several children who were molded excellently by his wife into ideal children. No one ever thought them wealthy as both Estrada and his wife decided early in their life to live modestly. He had a house that was large, but didn't stand out, as it always needed painting, and the yard was not significant. However, inside it could match Maximilian's palace. This is exactly what they wanted.

Estrada took Chanel into the inner workings of his business. She was extremely loyal to Estrada and he had tested her without her knowing. She now controlled the central bookkeeping. He paid her five times what normal business men made. She never disclosed this to her mother. Maria just thought she was a normal bookkeeper.

Chanel acquired a building made of concrete that sat apart from other buildings. It was a medium size building. She had a contractor build a jail cell inside and chains to keep someone from moving if they were locked in the chains. The cell had a vertical six inch pipe that lead to a sewer in the cell so that a person could relieve themselves and their waste. A lead pipe with a faucet was beside the pipe to wash away the waste toward the main sewer. It was fed by a tank some distance away.

There was nothing else in the cell, no chairs or beds, just a concrete floor, walls and ceiling. It did have a small window that was only six inches high and seven feet off the floor. Chanel had planned all this for Diaz. It gave her great pleasure building it with Diaz in mind.

The second night he was there, he came into Chanel's bedroom late at night as he wanted her. However, she knew he would try this and had paid two men to tie and gage him, then take him to her cell.

As Diaz came into the room with a evil leer on his face he was accosted by the two men who quickly had him bound and gagged. They threw him into the cell and locked the cell door.

After the men had left, Chanel entered the building and lit a lamp. She said, "Welcome to the rest of your life, Jamie. The only sex you will ever have will be with yourself. I am going to keep you here until you die. I will feed you, but not too much. I want you to live for years in here.

She then left and returned the next day when it was light. She had a half loaf of bread with her and threw it into his cell. He was very hungry, and picked up the bread and devoured it. He then cursed her, and she just smiled at him.

He was so mad that when she left he was shouting. The next day he had worked on the faucet and had managed to take it off the pipe, so that his cell was flooded.

When Chanel came that afternoon she said, "I'm not going to fix your faucet, you will have to sleep in the mess it made. There was a valve outside the building and she turned the water off. Now, Diaz had no water. She came twice a day to give him a little bread. He was hungry all the time. Now he was so thirsty that he could barely talk.

Chanel said, "If you will fix your faucet, I will give you a little water. He quickly placed the faucet back on the treads and turned it until it was in place. She went out and turned on the water, then walked back into the building. The water took a time to appear, then Chanel went back out and turned it off again. Diaz had only taken three swallows and was now sucking on the faucet.

Chanel said, "If you ever touch that faucet again, I will let you die of thirst."

Diaz said, "I won't, I promise. Please let me have more water."

Chanel said, "I'll think about it tonight."

The next morning when Chanel came to give him his daily supply of bread, Diaz was lying on the floor next to the faucet. Chanel said, "I will turn on the faucet for you."

Diaz pulled himself up and put his lips to the faucet. She just turned the valve a little so that only a few drops came out. Diaz licked the drops. Chanel said, "That is all until this afternoon. Diaz was sucking on the faucet when she left.

That evening she turned the faucet back on. She said, "I hope you learned your lesson, Jamie." Diaz nodded and said,

"I will never do anything again, I promise. How long are you going to keep me here?"

"Until you are a good boy, Jamie, and that may be a long time."

"I'm starving to death, can't you feed me more?"

"Yes, I think you diet needs to change."

The next day she brought fresh vegetables. There were two summer squash, some okra and an onion. She said, "These will be good for you. However, I remember you hated vegetables. I think you will learn to love them."

Diaz devoured them like a hungry hog. Chanel watched and said, "I see you have acquired a taste for vegetables, so that will be your diet while they are in season.

It was now turning cold and Carlos asked if he could have a blanket. Chanel thought maybe he would die from exposure if he didn't have one. She went to a place that sold dogs. She asked the owner if he had a blanket that was infested with fleas. The man grinned and said, "All my blankets are infested with fleas." Chanel bought one and put it in a sack and brought it to Diaz. It stunk like dogs and had fleas all over it.

Diaz was kept busy killing fleas for a few day. His diet had changed to raw potatoes, beets and carrots. Occasionally Chanel would throw in some bread.

Diaz had lost his fat stomach and most of the fat he had. He was now slim, but his beard was now streaked with gray. He had aged some.

Chanel could tell he was becoming addled so she decided to bring him a magazine. She held it up and said, "You must beg for this magazine, Jamie. Get on your knees and beg."

Diaz immediately got on his knees and begged. She then throw the magazine through the bars.

It was summer again and Carlos was looking very poorly. Chanel had spoke to a one of the women who worked for her as she knew she was married. She said, "I want to pull a trick on someone. Ask you husband if he knows any homosexuals."

The woman said, "You better think about that. You may make a permanent enemy of the one you are pulling the trick on."

Chanel said, "I don't think so, she likes that sort of thing."

The next day her friend said, "My husband really laughed when I told him of your request. He said he knew this one guy that had come on to him once. My husband said he is a big man. Here's his address."

Chanel looked up the man. He was big. Chanel said, "I will pay you fifty pesos to do something for me."

He grinned and said, "Who do I have to kill."

She smiled and said, "It is a tricky thing. I want you to have sex with a man that I am holding. Will you do it."

"If he's clean, I will do it."

"He will be clean, although he is being held for a crime he committed. He is in a special cell as he raped a small girl numerous time."

The next day Chanel said to Jamie, "I have brought you some soap and a towel. I have also brought you two nice blankets and some clean clothes. If you will clean up and smell nice, I will bring you someone you can have sex with."

Diaz said, "You're not just teasing me, are you?"

Chanel went back outside and brought the things she promised and left. The next morning when she threw him his raw vegetables, he looked clean and was in the clean clothes. Chanel said, "You will have your sex, Jamie, after all, I know how you love sex." Diaz just grinned.

That night Chanel went by the man she had engaged and said, "I want you to work up a sweat. I want you very sweaty when I take you to the man."

It went down just like she wanted. The man she engaged came into the jail cell and Diaz backed up to the back wall in terror. Chanel opened the cell door and let the man in, then locked it again.

The man said to Diaz, "Take off your clothes or I will take them off for you."

Diaz took off his clothes while the man was laying out the blankets on the floor. The man then pointed to the blankets and Diaz came meekly over and laid down. Chanel watched as Carlos yelled at first. It only took a few minutes. The man pulled up his pants and Chanel let him out. As he passed by her she noticed he smelled terribly. After the man left, Chanel said, "Now you know what it's like to be raped. I think I will get three or four to work on you the next time."

She did and Diaz was made to use his mouth on one while the other used his rear. Chanel didn't watch this.

The man she had arranged for this said, "My buddies liked that. They say they will be available anytime you want."

"No, I don't want him to begin to like it. He may switch to your kind."

The next morning Diaz wouldn't speak to her. He was in a corner sitting with his arms around his legs."

"Is your butt hurting, Jamie? Mine use to hurt when you

used me that way. I just hope those men didn't have any diseases." Diaz still didn't say anything.

Jamie now only weighed about a hundred and ten pounds. He was skin and bones. Chanel decided to feed him a lot of fat. She brought him meat that was ninety percent fat. It was cooked and Carlos ravished it.

A very large woman who lifted sacks all day was noticed by Chanel when she was walking. The woman was very strong. Chanel talked to her and they talked of men. The woman's name was Claudia. She stood six-two and weighed over two hundred pounds and there wasn't any fat on her.

Claudia said, "I like men, but they are intimidated by me. My father made love to me when I was ten and continued to do it until I put a knife through his neck. After that I grew to what you see now. I like to get small men, and make them do what I want them to do."

Chanel said, "I have a man who fits what you want. I will give you a hundred pesos to take him as you lover. Make him do things he doesn't want to do and if he resists beat him until he does. I want you to completely dominate him. I will put you on a boat at Lake Chapala for a week. I want him to be completely in submission to you when you return."

Chanel came to the cell and said, "I have some good news for you, Jamie. I have sold you to a woman. She wants to take a honeymoon with you on Lake Chapala. How does that sound."

"Wonderful," Carlos answered weakly. When do I leave. When I say you leave. You are still my prisoner. I will take you tomorrow to have a haircut and a shave. She drew out a thin dagger. She said, "If you give me any trouble, I will put this blade into you."

The next day Diaz could barely walk, but he was able to get in and out of a carriage. He was shaven and had a nice haircut. She had provided some nice clothes for him and a suitcase with other clothes in it. They picked up Claudia and Diaz gave her a weak smile.

Claudia like Diaz. He was small and weak, just like she liked her men. They drove to Lake Chapala where the large boat was waiting. They went aboard and cast off. They only went out about a mile and anchored. That night after they ate, Claudia took Diaz to bed. She cuddled him and treated him like a man would treat a woman. Diaz was so starved for human contact, he fell in love that night.

He now took orders from Claudia like a scared puppy. She liked to see his frightened face, when she dominated him. He did everything she wanted, but she still beat him because she liked to. She wanted him completely dominated. Claudia began to like Diaz because she now had him like she wanted him.

At the end of the week they came to shore. Chanel was there waiting for them. She said, "Well, how did it go, Claudia." Claudia said, "I like him and he loves me. I think we should be married. It's a different kind of marriage. I will lead, and Jamie will follow. If he doesn't he will be sorry he didn't. I think he likes it that way."

Chanel was awed. She smiled and said, "I guess I changed you, Jamie."

"You did, and brought me the finest woman in the world.

She will be the man in our marriage and I the woman. I love to mind her and I'll do anything she asks."

Claudia said, "He'd better, or I'll beat him within an inch of his life."

Diaz walked off to tend the boat and Claudia said, "I can't take your money Chanel. Jamie is as close as I will ever come to loving a man. He does everything I tell him and likes it. You have made me a happy woman."

Sometime later, Sid passed Diaz on the street and didn't even recognize him as he was thin and was led by a woman. Sid heard the woman tell this man to stand outside and watch the horses, while she went in to tend to some business. He meekly stood and held the horses.

Diaz knew the man was Doctor Porter, but knew Porter didn't recognize him as he had changed so much physically. The woman returned and said harshly, "Get up on the buggy and don't dally. She helped the man up, and they drove off. Sid stood there and thought, *"Those two have switched rolls, she's the man and he's the woman."*

A woman walked up and said, "Did you know that couple?"

Sid said, "No, but they have switched rolls. She's the man and he's the woman."

She said, "Yes, do you think it will start a trend?"

Sid smiled and said, "Are you coming onto me, Sir?" and the woman laughed and said, "I may ask your mother for your hand in marriage."

Sid said, "If you want to call on me, I will ask my mother. She will look you over and make the decision."

The woman said, "I'll be around tonight at seven. Where do you live?"

"I live in Maximilian's palace, but don't let that intimidate you. My mother is very strict and will want to look you over."

"I'll be there at seven."

CHAPTER 18

CHANEL PEREZ

"When Sid reached home Maria was in the great room. Sid recounted what he had just seen that afternoon and the woman he had talked with. Maria said, "Do you think she was serious."

"I don't know, but if she comes, you act as my mother. Act as if I am your daughter and the woman is a man calling on her. We ought to have fun with this."

At seven Chanel came and was dressed in a beautiful gown. She had a large bouquet of flowers and was let in by a maid. Maria had dressed very matronly with her black hair combed straight back with combs in it. Sid was sitting in another chair.

Chanel handed the bouquet to Sid and turned to Maria and said, "I'm Chanel Perez and I met your son today on the street. He appealed to me so I asked to call on him."

"What are your intentions, young lady?"

"Oh, strictly honorable, Madam. I found your son handsome, and I wanted to know his family."

Maria said, "I will introduce you. He is Doctor Sydney Porter and I am his mother. Will you have a seat?" and she pointed to a soft chair."

Maria said, "My son is rather shy, and you are the first woman to call on him. Does your family live here?"

"Yes, I live with my mother, but it is only temporary. I intend to have a place of my own soon, one that is big enough for a family."

"Are You gainfully employed?"

"Yes, I have a good job as a bookkeeper, and have a nice pathway to be promoted."

"Well, you seem a worthy woman. I will not oppose you calling on my son as long as you are chaperoned properly. He has not see the worldly side of this life, as I have protected him. There are so many women who pray on innocent men like him, you know."

"I am aware of those kind of woman, and I assure you my intentions are honorable. I will not pretend to be a saint, as while I was in college I sowed some wild oats, but I assure you I have put those things behind me. I intend to do what is right from now on."

"Well, I approve of you and think you a well disciplined lady and will look forward to you calling on my son."

"Sid, do you want to see this lady again?"

"Yes, indeed. Senorita Perez, will you have a drink with us?"

"Yes, that would be nice." a maid was there and Sid asked, "What would be your pleasure?"

"I will have tequila with a twist of lemon if you serve liquor in your house."

"Indeed we do. I will have some white wine, Lupe."

Maria said, "I'll leave you children, alone. I see that I can trust Miss Perez."

After Maria left and their drinks were served, Chanel said, "I don't know how much of this is real and how much was put on."

"All of it Miss Perez. Maria keeps this house and I explained what happened today and thought it would be fun to play the part that we saw today. I will say, Maria is like my mother."

"Tell me about yourself, Miss Perez?"

"First, call me Chanel and I will call you Sid. Wait a minute, I know you, you tended my mother when she was sick, You're Doctor Porter."

"I don't remember your mother, but if you were there I would have remembered."

"I was there, but mother was suffering a spell, and you were so intent on saving her that you never saw me. I liked that. You are dedicated to medicine as I am business."

"How did you come to live in this palace?"

"I own it. The revolutionary, Carlos Mendez, bought it for me. We are friends and for awhile he could not own property as it would have been confiscated, so he bought it, and put the deed in my name."

"He must be a dear friend."

"He is. He helps many of the downtrodden. President Juarez pardoned him after that traitor Diaz was exposed."

"It may be hard for you to believe, but that man who acted like a woman today is Jamie Diaz. He is a broken

man, and now likes to be dominated by that woman who is his wife. A long story of which I do not want to go into."
"Hard to believe? It's impossible to believe. He is the most despicable person I have ever met."

"He was. Have you read that passage in the Bible where Jesus told Nicodemus he must be born again to enter the kingdom of heaven?

"Yes."

"Well, Jamie Diaz was born again so to speak. I don't know whether he accepted Christ, but he has been born again."

"I guess we can all change. I want to change, myself. I have done things to help other people that might be sinful. I have not prayed at length about it, as I should have."

"You have just described everyone who knows Jesus, Sid. I did something that was terrible, but it had wonderful results. I asked myself if it came from God, after the results came, but I cannot reconcile it. Maybe we should both enter a monastery."
"It would probably be good for both of us, but I would surely be kicked out as my love for women is too great."

"Are you a womanizer, Sid?"

"No, and I don't want to get into that. If we are married, I might tell you."

"Is that a proposal?"

"No, I have too much to settle before I can ever ask anyone to be my wife."

"You're a charming man. I want to know you much better. As a matter of fact I would like to know everything about you."

"That would entail you telling me everything about your life and I'm sure, with what you told me, there are things you do not want me to know about your life."

"There is, but if we become close enough I will tell you."

"I'm not sure I would tell you, but who knows maybe I will."

"We could become friends by telling of our past if we agree to no judgment."

"I'm not sure that is possible, but I'm willing to try. Why don't you tell me something about yourself that you are ashamed of, then I will tell you something that I think is as bad about me."

"This is a game, but also a way to know each other before we get in too deep."

"Do you want to get in deep?"

"Maybe, I have never met a man like you. I have not been that interested as I was focused on my business and other things. I will start. I was raped by my uncle at age ten. He continued raping me until I was twelve, when he left."

"Wow! You start out big. Well, I fathered a child for a middle aged woman, because she wanted to have a child, badly. I didn't love her or have any feelings toward her, except that she hid me and saved my life. I told her I would probably never see her again, but she said she just wanted a child. I slept with her, not just once, but several times to make sure she was pregnant."

"You did that out of gratitude and love. That made me love you a little bit. I will tell you another. I hated all men, because of my uncle. Later when I began to accumulate some wealth, I devised a plan to imprison my uncle. I put him in a cell I had built out of a concrete building. I kept him there for two years, starving him and making him eat vegetable which he use to hate. I just let him out a month ago. He was just a shell of a man then."

"I was a doctor in a prison. I had a nurse who became so scared during a prison riot that the only way I could see to calm her down was to make love to her. I left her and didn't know she was pregnant. I went to see her five years later and met my child. She wanted another child so I slept with her again and again left.

"Wow! You have out done me for sure. How do you have time to practice medicine." She laughed. "You will soon be called the father of our country. If we marry we will see your children everywhere."

"No, there are just the two and sometime later, three"

"Well, I guess it is my turn again. I imprisoned the man who raped me for two years. I hired a large homosexual and put him in the cage with the man. I watched as he raped him and enjoyed it."

"I guess we are both sexual people as everything we do is related to sex in one way or another. She was pregnant at the time and knew she was. She knew I was not in love with her and didn't want to hold me that way.

"After our clinic was up and running and we were making a good profit, I left. I returned five years later to find a four year old boy who was named Sidney Porter, Jr. I did not stay, but she talked me into fathering another child."

"I'm feeling I might be pregnant before the night is over," Chanel said.

"No, I only father children when there is a good reason and am asked."

"Well, I must go back to the uncle I had in my private prison. I later had that homosexual bring several of his friends to make my uncle perform all acts of sex with them. I never did it again after that time as I didn't want him to start liking it. The next day I saw him sitting in a corner of his cell drawn up and afraid. I told him that I knew his butt was sore as mine was when he did me that way."

"Let's tell some of the good things now before we shoot each other."

"I wouldn't shoot you. You did all the things you did out of love. You wanted to help people, whereas I wanted to destroy my uncle and thought I did. However, I met a woman who was about six-two and weighed over two hundred pounds and there wasn't an ounce of fat on her. She was raped as a child by her own father. She told me after two years she put a knife through his neck and had no remorse.

"She grew up where she would not go with a man unless she dominated the man completely. She found some men who liked to be beaten and dominated, especially when it came to sex. I gave her my uncle who now weighed only about a hundred and ten pounds. She took him to a boat on Lake Chapala and stayed with him a week. They fell in love as he now likes to be dominated. They were married. The couple you saw today was that couple. They love each other and my uncle does not have a dominate bone in his body. That man you saw is Jamie Diaz, and has been born again."

"My, that is a happy ending. Do you suppose he will ever leave her and start doing the things he used to do?"

"No, she told him about killing her father and he will stay in line."

"That is about all I have. Who can you tell me about that is not the mother of your children?"

"You, so far," and they both laughed.

She said, "You have slept with many women and I have never slept with anyone but my uncle. I don't know if I could ever submit to a man."

"That could be. It would have to be a man you had known a long time and that you respected. It would have to be a man who you grew to love, and wanted to be with him always. He must take his time and be very patient. It must happen over a long period of time."

"Are you thinking of yourself when you are laying out that criteria?"

"I don't know. Maybe, we know too much about each other."

"No, the stories we told ended well. I would like to see all your children together twenty years from now. I bet they would marvel that they were all sisters and brothers."

"I may do that, and if I do, I will be sure to invite you. Speaking of inviting, we have a fiesta here every Saturday night. I want you to come. Wear that gown you have on. It is lovely. You will wow the men who come. Maybe Carlos Mendez will come. You will like him."

Chanel stood and Sid showed her to the door. Sid said, "Shall I start your rehabilitation."

He took her in his arms and kissed her softly, then a little more passionately. As they stood back she said, "You are my doctor, now. I like your treatment. I will see you Saturday."

CHAPTER 19

A LETTER FROM MONTERREY

Dr. Contreras and Sid decided that they wanted more time off. Sid told the doctor about Teresa Lopez, his nurse, who was practicing medicine near Lake Chapala and he thought he could induce her to come practice with them.

Dr. Contreras thought it a great ideas. He said, "Some women are very reluctant to see a male doctor. She will help us with those women."

Sid wrote Teresa that he had a place for her in Guadalajara at his clinic. He told her that she would make more money, and that Sid, Jr. would get a better education.

She wrote back that she would accept his offer as soon as she could sell her business. She had hired a woman a year back, who knew medicine. The woman had the means to buy her out, so she gave her a good price.

Teresa worked out very well. The women who were reluctant to have a male doctor explore their privates, were glad to see a woman doctor. All the male doctors transferred those women immediately. The work load of the Sid and Doctor Contreras diminished so they lead normal lives, now.

Sid had kept up with Rafael and Clorresa and wrote them about every month. He received a letter telling that Senor Ramos was dying. Sid decided he would go see him.

The railroad had been completed between Mexico City and Monterrey so Sid packed up and left. He stopped in Mexico City to see Rico and the girls in a new play they were doing. He just spent one night and left the next day.

Adam was a darling and favored Rico. Salendra said, "When Adam is grown he will look exactly like him. At least we all hope he will."

On the train to Monterrey he slept most of the time. He had written Rafael and he and Cloressa were at the station to meet him. Sid immediately asked about Senor Ramos.

Cloressa said, "We told him you were coming, so he is holding on as he wants to see you. His mind is a little muddled at times, but he will remember you."

When they reached the ranch, Sid went immediately to see Senor Ramos. A large smile crossed Senor Ramos' face and he said, "Thank you for coming, Sid. I wanted to see you before I pass. I have always counted you as one of my sons."

He then winked at Sid and said, "You will soon have a clear path to Mama," and they both laughed.

Two days later he passed. It was not a sad time as they

celebrated his life. Hundreds of people came as he was loved by many in Monterrey. The priest said, "Heaven will be a little brighter now with Senor Ramos there. We will miss him, but many of us will join him soon."

Sid stayed a week. He was introduced to several young ladies, as Cloressa wanted to find him someone. Sid was polite, but quiet.

Sid took the time to ride over to Juanita's home. A little boy was playing out front as Sid dismounted. Sid handed the boy the reins as Juanita came out. She hugged Sid and said, "Carlos, I want you to meet your father."

The boy put on a huge grin and said, "Mama has told me much about you papa. My uncle also comes to see us some."

Juanita said, "He means my cousin, Carlos Mendez. He sends us money. Too much money, but he can afford it. We live very well. Maybe I have stretched the truth some, but I wanted Carlos to be proud of his father. I want to thank you again for giving me Carlos. He has filled my life with happiness."

"God gave you your son, Juanita. I only provided the means. I am proud of Carlos, too. He's such a happy boy. You have made him so."

"Are you married, Sid?"

"No, but I hope to be soon. I still practice medicine in Guadalajara and she lives quite close."

"I know she is beautiful. I hope you can make her as happy as you made me."

They had some cool water and talked for about two hours. Juanita told him many things about Carlos Mendez that he didn't know. He helped many widows and poor families.

Everyone knew of his generosity and he was wildly popular with the less fortunate.

Sid then stood and said, "I came to attend Senor Ramos' funeral mass. He was a close friend, and helped me out when I needed a friend"

"Yes, I heard of his dying. Everyone loved him. Hug me before you go."

Carlos was near, so Sid decided to kiss her goodbye so Carlos would know his folks were close. Juanita was very grateful for the kiss. Sid then picked up Carlos and said, "Always mind your mother, Carlos. She is very special."

Carlos clung to him and said, "I will, Papa. Please come see us again."

Sid said, "I will come, Carlos, audios."

After he was gone, Carlos came and hugged Juanita's leg and said, "He is just like you said, Mama. He loves us very much." Juanita smiled and said, "Yes, he does, Carlos, we must pray for him every day."

Carlos said, "I will, Mama."

The next day Sid took the train back to Mexico City. He had wired Rico when he would arrive and Rico and the girls were at the station to meet him. The girls all kissed him and they traveled to Rico's house. On the way Rico talked about the children. Sid could see he was very proud of them and a happy father.

Salandra said, "We all agreed to tell the children that Rico is the father of them all.. What do you think, Sid?"

"What else could you do. I think that is the best, as he is their father. I just hope that other children don't treat them poorly because of the plural family."

Tico said, "There are many bastard children in the city, because many men have mistresses. I think they will be able to handle it. The children love Angelica, our governess. The children all call her 'Lica,' and she is so good with them."

They had a party that night and Sid left the next day. He stopped in Tonala to see Julia. Her husband was there. He was unshaven wearing a dirty undershirt. He appeared half drunk. Julia introduced Sid as Doctor Porter from Guadalajara. She said, "Dr. Porter stops here on his way to and from Mexico City and is a valued customer. He bought that pistol that will fit under a coat."

Her husband gave him a toothy grin and the turned to Julia and said, "I'm out of tequila."

She said, "I have a bottle in the cupboard on the right-hand side."

He left and Sid said, "How do you put up with him?"

"He doesn't bother me anymore as his new woman is tequila. He doesn't eat much anymore, so I see him leaving us in a few years."

"I don't want to wait a few years. I need you."

"We will have to wait. It will be in God's timing."

Sid left despondent. He went to the diner and ordered a brandy to wash the taste of Julia's husband out of his mouth.

Saturday night they had a fiesta as usual. Chanel was there wearing a beautiful gown. Several of the men tried to talk to her, but she said, "I am here with someone," so they left her alone. She came and sat by Sid and told him that she had told the men that she was with him."

Sid smiled and said, "You are with me."

After the fiesta ended and everyone was going home, Chanel said, "Shall we have a drink together?"

Sid said, "Yes, but not here." He pulled her up and they went to his bedroom. He sat her on the soft coach in front of the fireplace. He then turned and fixed them a brandy in some snifters. He handed her the snifter and then sat beside her."

"Are you going to seduce me, Sid?"

"No, you would just end up pregnant and that's no good unless we loved one another."

She smiled and said, "After all the children you fathered, what's does one more matter?"

"To you, a lot. You have a career to think of, and a child would not fit into those plans. If you remember, I'm promised to someone."

"Oh, yes, Julia. She has a husband that probably uses her every night. Doesn't that bother you?"

"No. He's now married to a bottle of tequila, and doesn't bother her anymore."

"That's what she tells you."

"I've met him and can see he is an alcoholic."

"I can see I'm getting no sex from you tonight. I need to catch you when you're in a more vulnerable mood. I haven't given up hope of having you one night."

"Just one night?" Sid said with a smile.

"Well, maybe several times in that one night."

Sid didn't see Chanel for awhile. He was really busy.

Dr. Contreras brought a message in to him. He said it was from a women who could not come to the clinic and had asked that Dr. Porter come. Sid put a few things in his bag and left. He found the address and knocked on the door.

Carlos Mendez answered the door and said, "I'm sorry for the subterfuge, but Juarez is again out to get me. I thought I was through with that, but one of my people who works at the palace in Mexico City, saw the order. They knew where I lived. I knew the woman who lives across the street and we watched from her window. The soldiers came and searched my house. My maid later told me she had told them I went to Monterrey."

"Come to the palace you bought me. Everyone there can be trusted. You can live nicely there."

"Thank you, Sid. I have a favor to ask you. Will you go to Mexico City and talk with Juarez. Maybe you can shed some light on why he wants me."

"I will do that Carlos. I shall leave tomorrow."

"Before he left, Sid wired the President. The wire read: "I must see you as soon as possible. It is about Carlos Mendez."

When Sid arrived in Mexico City he went straight to the presidential palace. He was received by two soldiers who took him to Juarez.

The president invited him to sit down. Sid then said, "I was visited by Carlos Mendez yesterday in Guadalajara. He said you wanted him arrested, but does not know why."

"He has money that belongs to the state. We need that money. I am ordering you to take us to Mendez."

"I do not know where he is. He moves about. I never know where he is. He just shows up one day when I am eating at some restaurant or when I am at my clinic. His visits are at his choosing.

"Unless you cooperate, I will hold you here."

"I am cooperating. I surely didn't need to come to Mexico

City. Holding me will not help the situation, it will do just the opposite."

"Juarez just turned to one of the soldiers and said, "He is under house arrest. He is not to leave the palace unless I say so. Put him in one of the guest room on the second floor. That is all Doctor Porter. When you give us the location of Mendez you will be free to go."

"I just told you, I have no idea where he is."

The soldiers took him away. His room was nice and he had a valet that Sid assumed was to guard him, also. He was fed lunch at a large table with several other people. Most of whom ate in silence. There was a woman next to him that asked, "Are you under house arrest?"

Sid said, "Yes, are you?"

"Yes, they think I know where Carlos Mendez is, but I have no idea."

"Are you his woman?" Sid asked.

"She said, "One of many, probably. We have known each other for several years. I once thought he was going to marry me, but now I see I was only one of his many women. What is your relationship with Carlos?"

"I'm just a friend."

"Are you Dr. Porter?"

"Yes. How did you guess that?"

"Carlos talked a lot about you. You are a dear friend of his."

"Yes. We are good friends, but that is why I am here. The president thinks I know where he is. He doesn't realize that Carlos is like a ghost. He moves about like he pleases. Juarez could never catch him, as he has too many friends. Many in the presidents own guard are loyal to Carlos. To know him is to be loyal to him."

"Yes, I can see what you mean. I love him, but so does many other women."

They finished their meal and went back to their rooms. On the way back Sid learned that the woman's name was Valeria Costa. Her room was next to Sid's room, so he invited her in.

They had comfortable rooms with a fireplace, a couch and soft chairs. Maximilian had the palace built and spared no expense. Sid found some brandy and they had a drink. As they talked Sid could tell Valeria was about his age. She told him she had been married, but her husband was one of Carlos' men and had been killed. Carlos felt badly about her losing her husband, so he comforted her, and she gave him her love.

Sid asked, "I wonder how long Juarez plans on keeping us?"

"I think some of the reason is that the president likes young people like ourselves to eat with him in the evening and brighten up this place. There are several other women and another man. He is a musician who plays the piano. Juarez loves piano music and I think he is holding Jamie, mostly because he likes to hear him play."

"So this is a social arrest?" and they both laughed.

Valeria said "I see we have a common bath between our rooms. I think Juarez might have planned that. The doors to the hallway are locked at night. However, we can visit one another so we don't get lonely. Are you married?"

"No. I'm a widower. My wife died a couple of years ago. We had no children. Do you have children?'

"No. My only lover is Carlos. I am told he can have no children. If he could, half the country would be filled with his children." and they both laughed.

They heard the door to the hallway being locked. Valeria looked at Sid and said, "We are alone now. I want to bathe." She then got up and went to her room. Sid just kept sitting on the coach drinking his brandy.

In just a few minutes he heard water running. After just a few minutes more, Valeria stuck her head around the door and said, "The bathtub is huge, why don't you bathe with me."

Sid Thought, *"I surely don't want to get mixed up with this woman. After all, she's Carlos' woman by her own admission."* So he said, "Thank you, but I prefer to just drink my brandy tonight."

He then thought, *"It may be a disappointment for her tonight, but tomorrow she will be glad I declined."*

She bathed and put on her night clothes and a robe and returned. Sid refilled her glass with brandy

She said, "Most men would have bathed with me. Why didn't you?"

"One, you are Carlos' woman, and two, I have a sweetheart, that I try to stay true to."

"Well, I am Carlos' woman when he is about, but I know he philanders and so why not me? I understand a person having a sweetheart. She must be very dear to you."

"She is. Someday we will wed."

"I guess I will go to bed alone tonight. Goodnight."

Valeria left and Sid finished his drink. He marveled at his will power. The brandy had wanted him to go with her, but he thought of several consequences."

They were wakened the next morning by a knock on their doors followed by a voice that said breakfast is served. There were several at the breakfast table, and they exchanged names. All were under house arrest for several reasons. None mattered too much in Sid's way of thinking. He thought that Juarez had them there for his entertainment, although he only ate with them at night and then, only a few times a week. Always Jamie Foxx played the piano.

Several of the women eyed Sid. He would just smile at them. Evon Avoca came and sat on the other side of Sid as Valeria was sitting by him. Evon said, "I have wanted to talk to you about a private matter. Could you meet me tonight? I am just across the hall from you."

"They lock the doors at eight, so if we are going to talk, we must go now." He glanced at Valeria and could tell she didn't like it, but she didn't say anything.

When they got to Evon's room she said, "I understand you are a doctor?"

"Yes. May I help you?"

"She said, "This is a sensitive matter. I had sex with man and think he may have infected me. Can you check me and see if I am infected?"

Sid said, "Yes, but I usually have a nurse with me when I check a woman."

"Yes, but I don't want anyone to know but us, and I understand that doctors are confidential about peoples health problems."

"We are. I will check you, but I need good light."

She said, "I will bring a lamp close for you."

Sid said, "You only need to take down your skirt and undergarments."

"No, I want you to check me all over. I haven't been checked in sometime and I want you to go over ever inch of my body after you check my privates."

She disrobed then brought over the lamp. Sid checked her thoroughly and said, "You have a small infection, but I believe it will clear up in a few days. I will look at you again in a couple of days."

He then went over her body very thoroughly as she pointed out a couple of moles that had worried her. Sid told her they were nothing to worry about and that she appeared to be in good health."

Evon said, "I could see Valeria was not thrilled with you coming to my room. Tell her that I was worried about those moles and that was all it was."

They had not been gone that long, and returned to the dining room. Jamie had just concluded his concert, which he loved to give. Two of the women adored him.

Evon did not return to the coach and Sid leaned over and said, "Evon was worried about a couple of moles that had turned dark and wanted me to check them. They were nothing and now she is free from worry."

"I thought she wanted to show off her beautiful body to you."

"Well, she did that, also, but made no advances toward me."

They returned to their rooms and were locked in. Valeria said, "As long as we are locked in, I would like you to go over my body. I haven't had a checkup for two years. Let me bathe first."

She bathed and then stuck her head around the door and said, "I will be on my bed. Sid examined her. He said, "You are very healthy and have a beautiful body"

"I wanted you to see all of me. I didn't want you thinking of that Evon all night."

Sid laughed and said, "I see women everyday at my practice. Some are nice looking and others not so nice looking. I try to keep a professional view. It's late and I need to go." She didn't press him and Sid left."

In the middle of the night, he heard the outside lock being turned. He sat us. He had left a lamp turned down, but it was still light enough to see. The door opened and a woman came and said, "Get dressed. You're getting out of here."

Sid just did as he was told, and dressed and followed the woman. They passed a guard and he just smiled as they went by. At a side door they passed another guard who opened the outside door. It was raining. There was a carriage waiting, and Sid stepped in, but the woman didn't enter the coach, she just said, "Go," in a quiet voice.

They left at a walk and traveled for awhile at a walk. The speed then increased and they were now traveling down another street. It was now raining harder. They went down one of the main streets, and then onto the open road. They traveled several miles.

After two hours they pulled into a way station. The driver's helper opened the door of the carriage and said, "We are changing coaches. This coach must go back. Please step inside the station."

Inside was a table with hot food on it. Sid sat down and the diver and his helper sat with him. They all ate, then went to the door and another carriage was waiting. Inside they had prepared a bed for him. Sid knew he wouldn't sleep, but he could at least rest.

As it was pitch black because of the clouds, Sid had no way of knowing which direction they was traveling, so he just laid back and tried to rest.

He must have gone to sleep because it was now morning and they were pulling into a village. They turned down a street and traveled a few blocks, then stopped in front of a large house. The door opened and Sid stepped out and followed the driver into the house.

They went to a dining table with hot food on it. At the head of the table was Carlos Mendez. He said, "Buenos dias, my friend. Did you travel well?"

"Yes, but now I'm afraid Juarez will be wanting me, also."

"No, I have that covered. The guards will tell Juarez that Diaz kidnapped you."

Sid laughed and said, "You cover all the angles, my friend. You must have thousands of friends."

"I do. I have found that friendship is the greatest of all of God's gifts. Juarez, will know the guards are lying, but won't do anything to them as others may take his life and he knows that."

"I will take you back to your palace in a day or two and you can return to work. Juarez will do nothing to you.

"Sid, Maria said you told her you had a true love, but she is married to an alcoholic. I had a priest to annul that marriage. I bought the store and her husband is now in a place he can drink himself to death if he wants. I bought the store at a very high price on the condition he agree to the annulment. He did, and she is free. She is now at your palace."

Sid was overwhelmed, but he corrected Carlos and said, "Our palace."

Carlos said, "Yes, I am in partnership with hundreds of people and a few husbands," and they both laughed.

Sid said, "I met one of your women, at the palace in Mexico City. Her name was Valeria. Costa."

Carlos said, "Yes. When I heard you were under house arrest I had her placed so you had connecting rooms. I hope she gave you comfort."

"I didn't bed her as I knew she was your woman."

"You are such a loyal friend, Sid. I will never have a dearer friend. Are you going to get married now?"

"Yes, thanks to you. I have wanted to marry her since the first time we met. I think she felt the same."

"Sid, I want you to take her to New York City then to Paris on your honeymoon. I will see to everything. I will even have a valet to do all the business, so you are not bothered with that as you travel. It is my wedding gift."

When Sid reached the mansion, Julia was sitting on a couch reading. When she saw Sid, she ran to him and they embraced. She said, "Did Carlos tell you about the annulment?"

"Yes. Sit down I need to tell you some things before we wed."

As Sid's face was serious she sat and looked at him. Sid told her first about Teresa and their son, Sid, Jr. He explained it the best he could and why he bedded her.

"Have you ever seen a puppy tremble because it was so scared. It is a terrible sight. That is the way Teresa was. She trembled like that. I knew the only way to take her out of that state was to bed her. It took awhile, but it worked. She held me all night and would not let me go. I am not ashamed of what I did, as I think it may have saved her life. I know she treasures little Sid."

He said, "That's not all. When I was captured by Diaz and taken to Monterey, I escaped. I was hidden for a week by a middle aged woman. She was not comely at all. I asked her if there was anything I could do for her. She asked me to father a child for her. She was near the end of her childbearing years. I wish you could see the pleading in her eyes. She had risked her life to save mine. I wanted to do something for her and that is what she wanted, so I slept with her. Our union worked, and she had a child. She named it after her cousin, Carlos. He is a fine boy and I'm glad I helped Juanita have him.

"If you want to call off our wedding, I wouldn't blame you."

Julia came into his arms and said, "That just made me love you more, Sid. I hope I can give you many children. I want to take them to see their brothers and become part of their lives. You are special, Sid."

Julia and Sid were married and they traveled to New York City and stayed a week and saw a lot of shows. Their valet took care of everything.

They then went to Paris and stayed two weeks. They were deliriously happy.

They returned to Guadalajara and made the palace their home.

Rico came with his wives and children. They were very impressed.

Sid was telling Rico, "When you decide to give up show business, I want you and your wives to live here with us. Both Julia and I want to enjoy your children and see them grow up."

Rico said, "We will do that. I wish my sister could have seen these children, she would have loved them."

"I know she would. You surely miss her don't your, Rico." He nodded.

Teresa now lived in the mansion. She now had two children. Sid, Jr. and Dominic.

Sid made arrangements for Juanita to bring Carlos to live with them. They did and were all happy.

Sid told Julia, "You are the most understanding wife in the world."

"That is because I love you unconditionally and have you every night. You have made me the happiest woman in the world."

They had several children. The other children thought of their children as their brothers and sister. Sid continued his work at the clinic with Teresa.

Julia met Chanel Perez and they became great friends Chanel now owned the business her benefactor had given her. He was in poor health and moved to Mexico City.

Chanel talked Julia into helping her and the business expanded.

Carlos Mendez came by many times and the warrant that Juarez had on him was cancelled. Carlos was always the life of the party when he attended the fiesta. He even brought Valeria. She was now his woman, most of the time.

The End

Printed in the United States
By Bookmasters